Sherlock Holmes
The Picture of Innocence

AIRSHIP 27 PRODUCTIONS

Sherlock Holmes The Picture of Innocence
© 2016 Chuck Miller

Cover illustration © 2016 Mal Earl
Interior illustrations © 2016 Rob Davis

Editor: Ron Fortier
Associate Editor: Fred Adams Jr.
Production and design by Rob Davis
Promotion and marketing by Michael Vance

Published by
Airship 27 Productions
www.airship27.com
www.airship27hangar.com

ISBN-10: 1-946183-03-2
ISBN-13: 978-1-946183-03-3

Printed in the United States of America

10 9 8 7 6 5 4 3 2 1

SHERLOCK HOLMES
"The Picture of Innocence"

by Chuck Miller

FOREWORD

recently prepared for publication, under the title *A Confederacy of Devils*, an account of one of the early adventures of the Bay Phantom. In this, I was aided by Janie Marie Colson, executrix of the estate of the late Joseph Perrone of Mobile, Alabama. Last year, Ms. Colson informed me that she had recently come into possession of an old steamer trunk filled with documents and other interesting artifacts that had once been the property of the late Mirabelle Darcy. Among these, Ms. Colson discovered a manuscript titled *Sherlock Holmes and the Picture of Innocence*, which purported to be an unpublished tale by none other than John H. Watson, M.D.

How Mirabelle Darcy came into possession of this account, we do not know. As readers of the first Bay Phantom book are aware, Ms. Darcy was a very extraordinary woman, who corresponded over the years with a great many prominent people. It is possible that one of them was Sir Arthur Conan Doyle; she may even have been acquainted with Watson and Holmes themselves. The manuscript is dated 1940, some 10 years after Conan Doyle's death, so he could have had no involvement in its production.

The manuscript is hand-written, and is remarkably legible when one considers that Watson was both a doctor, and was almost 88 years old when it was produced. I had little trouble transcribing and editing it for publication. Ms. Colson had the pages tested at a private laboratory in New Orleans. I have before me a detailed report that states unequivocally that the paper and ink are of the correct age.

Watson obviously intended to publish it. Why he did not is a question I cannot answer. Perhaps he passed away before he could begin the process. The date of his death is in some dispute; William S. Baring-Gould places it on July 24, 1929. If he is correct, the current manuscript is obviously a forgery. However, an exhaustive search of a number of online databases has failed to turn up any record of the death of John H. Watson in 1929, or any other year. His final fate, like that of his friend, Mr. Sherlock Holmes of Baker Street, is officially unknown.

If Watson was in London in 1940, it is possible that he was one of the unidentified victims of the series of German bombing raids known as the Blitz. Personally, I prefer to think that he made it out of the city before the bombs began to fall, and that he spent his remaining years in some green and pleasant place. The Sussex Downs, perhaps, where he would have enjoyed the best of company and all the honey he cared to consume.

Chuck Miller
Norman, Oklahoma
2015

INTRODUCTION

y friend, Mister Sherlock Holmes, has become a celebrated figure, thanks in no small part to the efforts of myself and the late Sir Arthur Conan Doyle. To this day, Holmes claims that his status as a near-legendary figure is an annoyance to him, but I believe he is secretly delighted. Motion pictures, which still seem to me a very strange new storytelling medium, have taken him up with enthusiasm. The actor Basil Rathbone is very like my old friend in many ways. I must say, though, that I am less than thrilled with Nigel Bruce's interpretation of my own character, but I have to admit that it is effective from a dramatic standpoint.

I am almost 88, and I have no doubt that my time on this earth will soon draw to a close. My hearing is very poor, and I am all but immobile, thanks to age and my ancient war wounds. But my mind is, so far as I can determine, sharp and unclouded. Certainly my recollection of certain events in the autumn of 1885 are quite clear. For the past week, I have been meticulously reviewing the copious notes I kept during that period, many of which were incorporated into the almost-entirely fictional novel, *The Sign of the Four*. Yes, at long last, I admit that some of the chronicles that Doyle and I presented to the reading public—but only a very few—were pure fiction, though they always contained at least a grain of truth.

Now that the end of my days is a close and inevitable presence, rather than some phantasm of the far-away future, I feel compelled to "set the record straight," as they say.

Faithful readers of the Sherlock Holmes stories will no doubt recognize some familiar elements from *The Sign of the Four* and *A Scandal in Bohemia* in the account that follows. I have before me the extensive notes I took at the time, which were later used to construct those two fabrications.

Readers may also discern echoes of another novel, *The Picture of Dorian Gray*, by Mister Oscar Wilde. The late author and playwright was a party to the strange doings involving the Agra treasure and the dark secret of the Sholto brothers. Literary historians may be discomfited by my account of Wilde's participation in events that would inspire his only novel. I can only assure them that what follows is the truth, however improbable it may seem.

Much has been said of Wilde, both good and ill, as a man and an *artiste*. I have nothing to add to the scholarly debates or the moralistic arguments, except to say that I found him a stout companion in adversity, and a delightful, if somewhat exhausting, conversationalist. There were few topics under the sun upon which Wilde could not discourse at length, displaying remarkable knowledge and effortlessly wry humour. Next to that of Holmes himself, Wilde possessed the most remarkable mind I have ever encountered. And, like Holmes, Wilde could be endearing and insufferable in equal measure.

Sadly, his uniqueness and contempt for convention helped him find his way to his spectacular and tragic downfall. I shall not dwell on the sordid details. I often think of him; the brilliant career in which he took such delight, the indignities he suffered thanks to his unfortunate relationship with the fatuous Alfred Douglas, and the devastating final act: imprisonment, disgrace, physical ruin, exile, and death. He could have quite easily avoided that denouement, but seemed determined to rush headlong to his own undoing. I cannot explain that, except to say that he struck me as a man whose entire life was a desperate search for something he could not name or describe. In this, he reminded me again of Holmes, whose professed devotion to logic and reason was but a self-manufactured illusion with which he attempted to fill some large, empty place in his soul.

Holmes was more fortunate than Wilde—indeed, he is alive and remarkably active even as I write these words, his reputation not merely unsullied, but grown to the status of legend within his own lifetime—but the two men had much in common: They were too brilliant and too fiercely unconventional for their own good. Each was obliged to forge his own unique place in the world of ordinary men and woman, blazing trails that few others would dare follow. And it took a toll on both of them. Holmes survived and prospered, but could never completely cast off the deep and perplexing sense of alienation and sorrow that has been his most constant companion in life.

Wilde allowed his personal darkness to destroy him. Some say he abetted it, perhaps unconsciously, and there may be truth in that. I cannot say. I am something of a dullard, I suppose—and quite content with my lot. I do not have the fortitude to contend with the sort of demons that plague men like Holmes and Wilde, and I would never presume to pass any but the mildest of judgments upon them. I often scolded Holmes over his use of cocaine, while acknowledging to myself that the alternative might be worse. I looked askance at certain of Wilde's proclivities, but I was more concerned with the danger they posed to his life and liberty than with any supposed moral failing they might represent.

Readers will no doubt be shocked by some of the revelations contained herein, particularly those concerning Mary Morstan. Or perhaps, in this year of 1940, they will not. The world is changing rapidly, by which I mean the attitudes and activities of its inhabitants. There are a great many things we used never to speak about; now self-imposed restrictions are falling away.

The faithful reader will encounter familiar passages in new settings; and will, I hope, understand why the original deception was thought desirable.

There are aspects of the affair about which neither Holmes nor I ever learned the full truth. We drew reasonable inferences based upon what we *did* know, and I trust that the reader may do the same.

At the time these events were unfolding, I was puzzled by Holmes' peculiar conduct. It would be many years before I began to understand, and I have incorporated that understanding in this account.

And I will further state to the reader that what follows is not a typical Sherlock Holmes "adventure," though there are thrills and action enough for those who crave it. It is, rather, a chronicle of certain seminal events which, I believe, give valuable insight into the character of the man, and that of your humble narrator as well. It will, I hope, allow devotees of the Holmes "canon" to revisit those venerable tales with fresh eyes.

Doctor John H. Watson M.D.
London, England
1940

CHAPTER ONE:
Doctor Doyle

"I cannot imagine, Watson, that the reading public would show any enthusiasm over an account of one of my investigations," said Sherlock Holmes. "It might be appropriate matter for a specialized journal. The process by which I examine my data and arrive at my conclusions is purely scientific, and hardly the stuff of popular literature. One might as well pen a romance based upon the measuring of rainfall in a given area over a given span of time. I am an analyst, not a swashbuckler."

"I beg to differ, Holmes," was my adamant reply. "While it is true that you are essentially a scientist, you are also a man of action, and, if I may say so, a most fascinating character. I have described for Doctor Doyle some of your habits and, ah, eccentricities, and he is of the opinion that you would go over smashingly as a protagonist."

"Ah, yes, the redoubtable Doctor Doyle," Holmes said with just a hint of a sneer. "He is poised to take the literary world by storm, duplicating his spectacular success in the medical field, eh? How fortunate you are to have come under his influence!"

"Sarcasm does not become you, Holmes," I said sternly. "And you do the man a grave injustice. Doyle is a fine fellow, with quite a bit of talent."

"And, it seems, an overwhelming reluctance to display it in any way."

Holmes had, for reasons I could not fathom, taken a dislike to my friend and colleague, Doctor Arthur Conan Doyle, and all of this without ever having met the man. While it was true that Doyle's medical practice had not been a resounding success, it was hardly necessary to allude to it in such an insulting manner. It was my practice to give Holmes the benefit of every possible doubt, owing to the unique nature of his mind and personality, but his seemingly capricious attitudes could be most trying. Though he prided himself on being a disciple of reason, he frequently, and for reasons known only to himself, refused to listen to it.

"Really, Holmes," said I, "this is unworthy of you. You do not know him, and I cannot imagine what you have against him. I would be grateful if you would provide me with one of your logical, point-by-point explanations of the position you have taken with regard to him, because I confess I am baffled."

Holmes laughed and waved a hand. "I have nothing against him as such," said he. "But neither do I have anything *for* him. He strikes me as a man bent on making a name for himself, and none too particular about how he does it. In that way, he is, I suppose, my antithesis. I live for the work I do, and any fame I might achieve as a consequence is more annoyance than reward. I should much prefer to toil in obscurity, and perfect my craft without distractions. Detection is, or ought to be, an exact science and should be treated in the same cold and unemotional manner."

I scoffed at this. As I have mentioned elsewhere, Holmes had a broad streak of vanity in his character, and he delighted in the awe and admiration his abilities stirred in those around him. I did not know whether he intended me to take seriously his protestations to the contrary, or if he was indulging in a bit of ironic, self-deprecating humour. Either way, I had reached my limit.

"Where have you come by all this information, Homes?" I asked.

"None of it constitutes a state secret, Watson. I merely went places and asked questions."

"You spied upon him!"

"Watson, really! I made *inquiries*."

"Very well, then. And you were unimpressed with what you learned. What of your dictum regarding personal observation? Does it not behoove you as an investigator to gain first-hand knowledge of your subject?"

He threw his hands up and said, "You have me! You are a very cunning man, Watson, to turn my own words against me. Ask the fellow to come 'round and I will speak with him. Will that satisfy you?"

I allowed that it would, and the subject was closed for the moment.

Not long after Holmes had cleared up the mystery surrounding the murder of Enoch J. Drebber, I decided to try my hand at a volume of autobiographical sketches. Mister Sherlock Holmes was never meant to occupy a central role of the body of work I envisioned. After all, I reasoned, I had led an interesting and eventful life in my own right before I ever met the man who would one day be hailed as the Great Detective of Baker Street.

The bulk of my "opus" was dedicated to my doings as an assistant surgeon attached to the Fifth Northumberland Fusiliers during the Afghan War. I felt certain that my first-hand accounts of the military campaigns in which I had been involved were sufficiently gripping to attract a large readership.

I had included a brief sketch of my introduction to Holmes and his investigation of the Drebber killing, almost as an afterthought.

The Reminiscences of John H. Watson, M.D., Late of the Army Medical Department was privately printed in 1885, and proceeded to set world records for the lack of attention it garnered and the speed with which it was utterly forgotten by everyone but its poor author. I had sunk most of my remaining capital into the wretched thing, not to mention my self-respect, and the rewards had been nil.

It was in a mood of considerable dejection that I wandered one afternoon into the Criterion Bar. I had just visited my bank to sort out an embarrassing matter involving multiple overdrafts, and been sent away with a flea in my ear and my tail between my legs. So much for John H. Watson, Man of Letters!

And then there was my brother. Harry Watson had passed on not so very many months before, a victim of his own alcoholic excesses. Even now, it is painful to dwell on his sad and protracted decline. To put it succinctly, he had been left with good prospects after our father died, but the habits of a lifetime proved impossible to break. He threw away his chances, lived for some time in poverty with occasional short intervals of prosperity and finally, taking to drink, he died.

Our father, it must be said, was an inflexible, unforgiving man. Harry had realized early on that he could never live up to the man's expectations, and had given up trying. I, on the other hand, had done my utmost, but to little avail. The expectations in Harry's case were greater, he being the eldest son. But, as I came to realize, our father held up an impossible ideal. He himself had never achieved a tenth of what he expected from his sons, but that made no difference. He had gone to his grave cursing the barren ground that his progeny had become, never realizing his own fault in failing to sow the proper seeds.

And now, all I had left of poor Harry was the watch I had inherited upon his death. I took it from my pocket. It was a rather grim reminder of Harry's final years—and, indeed, of the many failures of the Watson family. I turned it over in my hand and wondered how much I might get for it from a jeweler. A reputable dealer might give me as much as fifty pounds for it, a not inconsiderable sum, and most attractive given my current financial straits. Shameful though it was, I gave the idea serious consideration. Finally, I put it back into my pocket. I still had an inexplicably strong sense of family honor, though I had no family left, and could not truthfully say that I had ever particularly honored them.

As I was washing down the lump of self-pity in my throat with a whiskey and soda, someone tapped me on the shoulder.

Turning round I recognized young Stamford (no longer quite so young as he once was), an acquaintance of mine whose first name I had never learned, and was now too embarrassed to admit it and ask him what it was.

"By God, Watson," he said jovially, "I seem to find you here every time I enter this establishment. Believe it or not, old man, this is the first time I have set foot in this place since I bumped into you four years ago. How have you been keeping, and how long did it take you to become fed up with Mister Sherlock Holmes?"

I had not set eyes on Stamford since 1881. On that occasion, our chance meeting in this very bar had culminated in my introduction to Sherlock Holmes, who, like myself, was looking for someone to share living expenses.

I gave him an abbreviated version of my doings since then. He was rather surprised to learn that Holmes and I still shared rooms.

"Still having a bit of financial trouble?" he inquired, not unkindly.

"I am afraid so," I replied. "I gambled what little I had managed to accumulate on literary success, and lost. I feel inclined to give up on the idea of being an author, and concentrate on building a medical practice."

Stamford laughed.

"My dear Watson," he said, "I believe we have been here before. *Deja vu*, I think it's called."

"How do you mean?"

"Just this: Once again, you are the second man that has expressed that very sentiment to me today."

"And this," said I, "is the second time you have spoken *those* words to *me!*"

"History does tend to repeat itself," he said.

"And as for today," I said, "who was the first man to use my expression?"

"An acquaintance of mine named Doyle. Doctor Arthur Conan Doyle. I don't know if Conan is his middle name or part of a compound surname. Probably the former, as I have not seen a hyphen anywhere near it. He, too, has literary ambitions that have thus far eluded him, and has been thinking of letting it drop and throwing himself wholeheartedly into his medical career. But he has the eternal problem, Watson: Money—the lack of it. Not to mention the fact that he was married recently. He is looking for someone to go halves with him on an office here in London."

I gave him a stern look and said, "Stamford, this is really too much. If you're having me on..."

"No, no, my dear fellow!" said he, with a laugh. "I swear by all that I hold dear, I am telling you the truth. I am as astonished by it as you are. And now, as is our custom in these situations, I had best take you to meet my acquaintance. I can assure you that he is a great deal less eccentric than the last chap to whom I introduced you."

We finished our meal, chatting about the few "old times" we had shared. Stamford very casually offered to pay my check as well as his own, and I very casually accepted. Nothing was said, nor did anything need to be. Stamford was indeed a rather fine fellow. I regret that I cannot, to this day, recall his given name.

Stamford accompanied me to Doctor Doyle's residence in Upper Wimpole Street. I learned that Doyle had been married quite recently, in August of that year. His wife was quite charming, though she seemed vaguely sad. There was also something about her that made me think her health was not all that it should be. She appeared hale enough, but I think physicians develop a certain sense about things, and mine told me that Louisa Doyle's life would not be a long one. And yet, there was something there that I envied.

Doyle had about him an air of easy amiability, coupled with a certain gravitas that was unusual in one so young—he was only six-and-twenty, as I would later learn. He was tall and solidly-built. I would almost describe his round face as cherubic, in spite of the drooping moustache he wore.

After Stamford had introduced us, Doyle looked me in the eye, smiled broadly, and shook my hand. "I say, you wouldn't happen to be the author of *The Reminiscences of John H. Watson, M.D., Late of the Army Medical Department*, by any chance?" He spoke with a noticeable Scottish burr.

"As a matter of fact, I am," I admitted. "And more's the pity. That book is part of the reason I find myself in my present situation."

He smiled ruefully and said, "Indeed, my dear fellow, you and I have drunk from the same bitter cup. My own literary efforts have met with little more than polite indifference."

"It could be," said I, "that I simply don't have the makings of a story-teller."

"Actually," said Doyle, "I found your account of your experiences in Afghanistan most gripping. However, if I may say so, there has been a perfect deluge of such memoirs in recent years, and yours may have been overlooked. But it was the latter part of the book that really caught my attention. This Mister Sherlock Holmes of yours is most intriguing. One seldom encounters such characters in real life. He reminds me a bit of Poe's Dupin."

"I expressed that very sentiment to Holmes once," I said. "His response was that Dupin was 'a very inferior fellow.'"

Doyle chuckled. "Well, I suppose he would have to think so. It would require a very... ah, robust ego to set oneself up in the sort of position your friend has. I should like very much to meet him and see how he operates."

"I don't see why not," I said. I had developed an immediate liking for this man, but I wished to spend a bit of time in his company before I committed myself to any business arrangements. Perhaps he felt the same way, for we did not discuss business at all that evening. I spun a few tales of wartime adventure.

Eventually, the conversation turned to the subject of my fellow-lodger.

"Lately," I said, "he can be heard from dawn until dusk, bemoaning the lack of interesting crimes."

"Really? One would hardly know it if one went by the *Pall Mall Gazette*."

"Oh, there is plenty of crime, right enough. But none of it is sufficiently exotic to absorb Holmes' attention. Only the most abstruse and impenetrable of riddles can fully engage him. The modern British criminal, it seems, is too straightforward for his taste."

I returned to Baker Street in an expansive mood. The excellent meal I had enjoyed at Doyle's house—not to mention the stimulating conversation—had lifted my spirits considerably. Holmes was absent, and I settled down in a chair near the window with a copy of the January 1884 *Cornhill Magazine*, which Doyle had given me; it contained a short story he had penned, "J. Habakuk Jephson's Statement." The tale, published anonymously, was a work of fiction based upon the curious circumstances surrounding the *Mary Celeste*, an American merchant brigantine which had been discovered adrift in the Atlantic Ocean in 1872. As the reader may recall, the captain and crew had apparently abandoned the vessel for reasons which were never discovered by investigators. None of the missing men were ever heard from again.

Doyle's story was, I thought, a very fine piece of work. I admired his ability to blend fiction and fact in such a way as to make the former seem plausible and of a piece with the latter. I read it through twice, from start to finish, and it was then that an idea took root in my head. I put the magazine aside and sat gazing out the window, examining my new-born notion and finding nothing wrong with it.

Nothing, that is to say, but an obstacle that might prove formidable, if not insuperable. I would have to give the matter considerable thought.

While I was thus occupied, Sherlock Holmes returned. He glanced at me and nodded as he removed his jacket and hung it on a peg.

"I trust that you enjoyed your supper at the home of your friend. A man of letters, eh?"

Though I had grown somewhat accustomed to Holmes' feats of seeming clairvoyance, they never failed to fill me with surprise and astonishment.

"However did you know what I have been up to?" I asked.

Laughing, he lowered himself into his armchair and lighted a cigarette.

"You have carelessly allowed a bit of gravy to drip onto your tie," said he. "While I cannot claim the ability to identify different kinds of gravy by sight, I know that Mrs. Hudson has not prepared anything resembling your stain in recent days. Of course, you could have dined out, but—forgive me for saying so—the state of your pocketbook argues against it. Thus, you have been a guest in the home of a friend. That he is a literary man of some sort is suggested by that copy of the *Cornhill Magazine* upon your lap. Though it is a popular journal, I happen to know that you are not a regular reader, based upon disparaging remarks you have made about it on several occasions. What, then, could induce you to bring a copy home with you? It seems probable that it was a gift from your host. And why would anyone make a present of a magazine more than a year old—that is, I believe, the January 1888 number—unless it contained a piece that he thought would be of particular interest? That he wrote it himself is, perhaps, a bit of a leap, but I can see by the expression on your face that I have hit my mark."

"Simple enough when you explain the thing," I said, "but all the more wonderful for it. I sometimes wish I could turn the tables and give you an account of your recent activities, but my powers of observation, as you frequently remind me, are quite pitiable compared to your own. So I must ask you what *you* have been up to today. Have you found any 'little problems' worthy of your attention?"

A sour expression passed over his face and he shook his head.

"I fear not," said he. "I am just now returning from Scotland Yard, where Inspector Lestrade presented me with what he assured me was a riddle fit to stump the Sphinx. I cleared it up for him in less than five minutes, without ever leaving his office. It frustrates me intolerably! Give me problems, give me work, give me the most abstruse cryptogram, or the most intricate analysis, and I am in my own proper atmosphere. But the criminals of London seem to be involved in a conspiracy to make their doings as transparent as a pane of glass. They are starving me to death, Watson!"

With that, he stood and stepped over to the corner of the mantelpiece, where he took a bottle and a hypodermic syringe from a neat moroccan case. With his long, white, nervous fingers he adjusted the delicate needle and rolled back his left shirtcuff. For some little time his eyes rested thoughtfully upon the sinewy forearm and wrist, all dotted and scarred with innumerable puncture-marks. Finally, he thrust the sharp point home, pressed down the tiny piston, and sank back into his armchair with a long sigh of satisfaction.

"Is that absolutely necessary, Holmes?" I asked, not bothering to disguise the disdain in my voice.

He glanced in my direction, a far-away look in his eyes.

"No, my dear fellow," said he, "strictly speaking, it is not. But it is desirable. Give me problems, give me work, give me the most abstruse cryptogram, or the most intricate analysis, and I am in my own proper atmosphere. I can dispense then with artificial stimulants. But I abhor the dull routine of existence. I crave for mental exaltation. And I find it in the cocaine-bottle when it is scarce on the ground in everyday life."

"You may believe all of that now. And you may revise your opinion when you have ruined your health."

"There is a certain risk, I'll admit. I accept it and will not blame anyone else should I come to grief. Your objections are noted, Watson, and I give you permission to remind me that you told me so, should the worst come to pass."

"That isn't my point, Holmes."

We lapsed into silence. Holmes stared off into space and I thumbed through my magazine. I fell once again to pondering the scheme I had so recently formed. It occurred to me that it might serve to divert Holmes'

"I fear not."

attention away from his ennui and the devilish solace it drove him to seek.

And there is, as they say, no time like the present. Our silence had lasted long enough.

"Well," I said, taking my opportunity, "since you recognized the magazine, perhaps you have deduced the identity of the man who gave it to me."

Holmes opened one eye. "I have not. I happened to recognize the cover; I have not committed its contents to memory."

"It would not have helped you, as the piece was published anonymously. Have you heard of Arthur Conan Doyle?"

"I have not."

"It was in his company, and his wife's, that I passed a pleasant evening. I told him of you and your work, and he found the whole thing most intriguing. He said you reminded him a great deal of a certain Doctor Joseph Bell."

This information was sufficiently intriguing to make Holmes open his other eye.

"Of Edinburgh?" he asked.

"Indeed."

"This friend of yours knows Bell?"

"I should say so. Doyle served him as a clerk several years ago at the Edinburgh Royal Infirmary. Am I to take it that you too are acquainted with Bell?"

"Mostly by reputation, though we did meet on one occasion. In what way do I remind your Mister Doyle of Bell?"

"*Doctor* Doyle, actually. And he said that your powers of observation and deduction are remarkably similar to Doctor Bell's."

"Obviously, Watson, you have something in mind, and I do not need my vaunted powers to deduce what it is. Allow me to give it some thought, and I will give you my decision in a few days."

And so, a few days later, we came to the exchange with which I opened this narrative. It would appear that I had my work cut out for me. But Holmes had, at least, agreed to meet Doyle, and that was something. When I was in the Army I learned to cherish small victories. Wars are won in increments, not all at once. I was content for the moment that the process of attrition had been set into motion.

CHAPTER TWO
Miss Mary Morstan & Miss Irene Adler

Doyle arrived promptly for his appointment, and introductions were made. Holmes received him cordially, and the three of us sat down, with mugs of tea supplied by our landlady, Mrs. Hudson.

"Doctor Watson tells me," said Doyle, "that you are dissatisfied with what one might call the quality of crime in London at present. I would think that the quantity would more than make up for any such failing."

"Were I a police inspector," said Holmes, "you would be right. But I am a different sort of creature. Give me problems, give me work, give me the most abstruse cryptogram, or the most intricate analysis, and I am in my own proper atmosphere. What am I to do with the thugs and hoodlums who perpetrate their endless crude burglaries and confidence games? I abhor the too-common tedium inherent in life. I crave for mental exaltation. That is why I have chosen my own particular profession, or rather created it, for I am the only one in the world. I cannot live without brainwork. What else is there to live for? What is the use of having powers, Doctor, when one has no field upon which to exert them? Crime is commonplace, existence is commonplace, and no qualities save those which are commonplace have any function upon earth."

Holmes seemed bent on dominating the conversation with his extravagant and self-absorbed complaints. I had opened my mouth to speak, with the intention of sparing Doyle any more of Holmes' tirade, when, with a crisp knock, Mrs. Hudson entered, bearing two cards upon the brass salver.

"Two young ladies for you, sir," she said, addressing my companion. "They have arrived unannounced, and unescorted, but they say that it is of the utmost importance that they speak with you."

Holmes took the proffered cards. "Miss Mary Morstan," he read. "And Miss Irene Adler. Hum! I have no recollection of either name. Ask the young ladies to step up." She nodded and went back downstairs.

"Don't go, doctors," said Holmes. "Watson, your presence has of course become invaluable. And, Doctor Doyle, these visitors may bring the sort of problem you are so keen to see me tackle. I've no objection to your observing our conference, if these ladies do not. Let us hope that it is something more intriguing than a lost kitten or a misplaced necklace."

Mrs. Hudson ushered two young ladies into our chamber and excused herself.

Mary Morstan was blonde and small, simply and rather cheaply dressed. She was comely enough, in a very wholesome, ordinary sort of way. Her dress was a sombre grayish beige, untrimmed and unbraided, and she wore a small turban of the same dull hue, relieved only by a suspicion of white feather in the side. Her expression was sweet and amiable, but a trifle forced, like a serving girl who was not at all certain about the security of her present position. In an experience of women which extends over many nations and three separate continents, I have seldom looked upon a face which held so little of the sort of promise I found intriguing.

Her companion was something else again. Miss Irene Adler was almost as tall as Holmes, and was in almost every way the opposite of Miss Morstan. Dark of hair and slightly swarthy of complexion, she was not quite what one would call a classical beauty, but there was something about her—a hint of darkness and danger that was most alluring.

"Miss Morstan, Miss Adler," Holmes said graciously, "It is a pleasure to meet you both. Do come in. I trust you will forgive the clutter. My associate and I are rather poor housekeepers, I fear."

He introduced Doctor Doyle and myself to the ladies and asked if they had any objections to our presence.

"I don't know how a pair of medical men could help us," Miss Adler said. "But I have never been known to turn away an attractive man, much less two of them."

Doyle's cheeks reddened and I am certain that my own did the same. Holmes, the extent of whose experience of women was unknown to me, seemed bemused.

He cleared his throat and said, "Do please sit down and tell me what I may do for you." He waved a hand at the basket-chair. "Just shift those papers out of the way, Miss Adler, and avail yourself of the cushion I assure you lies beneath them. Miss Morstan, please take the armchair."

Once the five of us were settled, Holmes favored Irene Adler with a languid gaze and spoke:

"You are from America, are you not?"

She nodded. "And how did you know that?"

"Your accent, of course. There is something in your vowels that insists upon New Jersey as your point of origin. You must have lived there for many years, at any rate."

"Right you are, Mister Holmes," she said brightly. "I was born there and spent—or rather *endured*—my childhood in Trenton."

Holmes nodded. "Well, since it is Miss Morstan's difficulty that brings you ladies here, and not yours, Miss Adler..."

"How do you know it isn't mine?"

"Because no one with a problem serious enough to impel her in my direction would ever be so glib as you are. By contrast, Miss Morstan's lip is trembling, her hand is quivering, and she shows every sign of intense inward agitation."

"Ah. I thought perhaps you had done something clever," she said. "The thing is very elementary, then."

"I never said otherwise, my dear Miss Adler. Do excuse me while I speak with your companion. Later, perhaps, you can tell me all about your career in opera. I am something of a musician myself, and I should like to hear your opinion of the Imperial Opera of Warsaw."

That seemed to take the young lady by surprise. Her eyes widened and she opened her mouth as though to speak, but she did not say a word.

"And now, Miss Morstan, state your case," said Holmes in brisk business tones.

"Well, it is because of Irene—Miss Adler—that I have come to you. That is to say, she suggested it."

"You once enabled a friend of mine, Mrs. Cecil Forrester, to unravel a little domestic complication," Irene Adler interjected. "Everyone was much impressed by your kindness and skill."

"I should hardly call a triple murder a *little complication*," Holmes said dryly, "though the solution was so astonishingly simple that the police overlooked it entirely."

"Nevertheless, Mister Holmes..."

Holmes held up a hand for silence, leaned forward in his chair, and spoke in carefully measured tones:

"I should be most grateful, Miss Adler, if you would allow Miss Morstan to state her case without further interruptions. I do not wish to seem brusque, but I assume that all of us present here are mortal, and we stand a better chance of getting to the essence of your visit before we reach the ends of our allotted spans if we are not distracted by interjections and asides."

He delivered this rebuke in a gentle, reasonable voice, with the sweetest smile on his face, and this caused Miss Adler to subside without protest, though she gave him a slight scowl. I foresaw more friction between the two of them if she continued her involvement in this matter.

"Well, briefly," Miss Morstan went on, "the facts are these. My father was an officer in an Indian regiment, who sent me home when I was quite a child. My mother was dead, and I had no relative in England. I was placed, however, in a comfortable boarding establishment in New Jersey—that is where Miss Adler and I became friends. I had distant relatives there, you see, on my mother's side. This was the reason my father gave for my relocation, though my relatives took very little notice of me. When I finished school, I remained in America for a time, as a guest of the Adler family.

"In the year 1878 my father, who was senior captain of his regiment, obtained twelve months' leave and planned to return to England. He telegraphed to me that he would arrive in London on a certain date, and directed me to come across at once, giving the Langham Hotel as his proposed address. His message, as I remember, was full of kindness and love. As it happened, Miss Adler was scheduled to perform with an opera company here, so we made the crossing together.

"On reaching London I drove to the Langham and was informed that Captain Morstan was staying there, but that he had gone out the night before and had not returned. I waited all day without news of him. That night, on the advice of the manager of the hotel, I communicated with the police, and next morning we advertised in all the papers. Our inquiries led to no result; and from that day to this no word has ever been heard of him."

"The date?" asked Holmes, opening his notebook.

"He disappeared upon the third of December, 1878; nearly seven years ago."

"His luggage?"

"Remained at the hotel. There was nothing in it save some clothes, some books, and a considerable number of curiosities from the Andaman Islands. He had been one of the officers in charge of the convict-guard there."

"Had he any friends in town?"

"Only one that we know of: Major Sholto, of his own regiment, the Thirty-fourth Bombay Infantry. The major had retired and lived somewhere around Belgravia. We communicated with him, of course, but he did not even know that his brother officer was in England."

"A singular case," remarked Holmes.

"I have not yet described to you the most singular part. Upon the fourth of May, 1882, an advertisement appeared in the *Times* asking for the address of Miss Mary Morstan, and stating that it would be to her advantage to come forward. There was no name or address appended. I had at that time just entered the family of Miss Adler's friend Mrs. Cecil Forrester in the capacity of governess. By her advice I published my address in the advertisement column. The same day there arrived through the post a small cardboard box addressed to me, which I found to contain a very large and lustrous pearl. No word of writing was enclosed. Since then every year upon the same date there has always appeared a similar box, containing a similar pearl, without any clue as to the sender. They have been pronounced by an expert to be of a rare variety and of considerable value. You can see for yourself that they are very handsome."

She opened a flat box as she spoke and showed us three very fine-looking pearls. I am, of course, no expert.

Holmes, on the other hand, was, and he examined them minutely, going so far as to employ his magnifying-glass. He turned the pearls over and over, one by one, uttering small, wordless exclamations.

"Yes," he pronounced when he had finished, "these are quite authentic, and rather fine. I would not venture to estimate their worth, but I am certain it is considerable. You might wish to keep them in a secure place rather than carrying them about with you.

"That is exactly what I have told her," Miss Adler put in. "She keeps them in a locked metal box under her bed, if you can believe it! I have told her many times that she should move them to a bank or some such place."

"Not a bad suggestion at all," Holmes allowed. "You might consider it, Miss Morstan."

"But that is not all," said she, ignoring Holmes' remark. "I have received a letter which has me somewhat puzzled. Irene thought there might be something sinister in it. That is why I have come to you. Here it is—you will perhaps read for yourself."

"Thank you," said Holmes. "The envelope, too, please. Post-mark, London, S. W. Date, July 7. Hum! Man's thumbmark on corner—probably postman. Best quality paper. Envelopes at sixpence a packet. No address, of course.

"*Be at the first pillar on the right outside the Lyceum Theatre to-night at nine o'clock. Come alone. If you do not, all will be in vain. Your unknown friend.*'

"Miss Morstan, you must not keep this appointment under the conditions stated. That would be foolish. The writer of this letter may well mean you no harm, but it would be pure lunacy to run such a risk. If you intend to follow through, I shall be very close at hand, as will Doctor Watson—and Doctor Doyle, if he wishes. Have you any objections to such an arrangement?"

"Of course not," Miss Adler said. She ignored the icy glare Holmes aimed in her direction.

"No," said Miss Morstan. "Though the letter contains no overt threat, it is certainly strange. There is safety in numbers."

"Indeed," said Holmes with a crisp nod. "Very sensible, Miss. There is one other point. Is this handwriting the same as that upon the pearl-box addresses?"

"I have them here," she answered, producing half a dozen pieces of paper.

"You are certainly a model client. You have the correct intuition. Let us see, now." He spread out the papers upon the table and gave little darting glances from one to the other. Doyle stood up and looked over his shoulder.

"They are disguised hands, except the letter," Holmes said presently.

"Handwriting is more difficult to disguise than most people would imagine," said Doyle.

"That is so," said Holmes. "There are certain traits which inevitably shine through. Hmm... Though there are several similarities, I feel quite certain that the recent letter was *not* written by the same man who addressed the pearl-boxes. See how the irrepressible Greek *e* will break out in both specimens, but the twirl of the final *s* in this letter bears no resemblance whatever to anything from the pearl-boxes."

"What does that suggest to you?" Doyle asked.

"One or two things," Holmes replied. We waited for a few moments, until it became plain that he had nothing to add to his remark. This was typical of my friend, and I had grown accustomed to it.

"I should not like to suggest false hopes, Miss Morstan," he went on, "but is there any resemblance between either of these samples and your father's handwriting?"

"Nothing could be more unlike."

"I expected to hear you say so. *Au revoir* then."

"*Au revoir*," said Miss Morstan. She replaced her pearl-box in her bosom. We made our arrangements; the ladies agreed to return to Baker Street at 8:30.

"Well," said Holmes after our visitors had departed, "what do you make of that pretty story?"

"I confess I am at sea," I admitted.

Holmes nodded, as though he had expected that answer. I rather supposed that he had.

"And you, Doctor Doyle," he said, turning to our guest. "Did Miss Morstan's tale suggest anything to you?"

"Perhaps," Doyle said. "But not enough to form any conclusions. I would have to know a great deal more before I could venture any conjecture."

"Indeed?" Holmes seemed impressed. "That is the very answer I was planning to give when one of you fired my question back at me." I felt an odd sense of satisfaction that my new friend seemed to possess a keener intellect than I did—or, at least, a greater ability to produce an answer that would meet with Sherlock Holmes' approval.

"Have you ever had occasion to study character in handwriting?" Holmes said to me. "What do you make of this fellow's scribble?"

He handed me the letter.

"It is legible and regular," I answered, feeling very astute. "A man of business habits and some force of character."

Holmes shook his head.

"A man of habits," he said, "but perhaps not business. Note the elaborate tails on the *y* and the *f*. Such flourishes are hardly necessary, and carry with them a suggestion of hedonism, it seems to me. Character? Men of character generally practice a certain economy of penmanship. I would say that our man is a creature of conflicting impulses. Look—there is some mild vacillation in his *k*'s, but there is self-esteem bordering on egoism in his capitals."

"You are able to discern all of that?" Doyle said wonderingly, taking the note which I proffered and scrutinizing it. "As far as I can see, it might have been written by anyone."

"I must admit that graphology is far from an exact science," Holmes replied, "but I have found from personal experience that one may make some reliable suppositions. You might wish to peruse the work of the Frenchman Jean-Hippolyte Michon and his disciple Jules Crépieux-Jamin. Some of their ideas are rather fanciful, but there is bedrock beneath them.

"Well, I believe we have wrung what we can out of these papers. We must add to our collection of facts before we venture into further speculation. That being the case, I propose that we concentrate our powers upon the excellent roast beef at Simpson's-in-the-Strand, and then apply our minds to an hour or two of Paganini as interpreted by the not-untalented Herr Ernst Junger at St. James's Hall, before accompanying Miss Morstan and Miss Adler on their most curious errand. What say you, doctors?"

We expressed our hearty approval of Holmes' scheme. Doyle said that he must first go home to his wife, and that he would meet us at Simpson's.

"Not such a bad fellow, Holmes," said I, after Doyle had gone.

"Well, he isn't an imbecile at any rate," my friend admitted. "Perhaps our business tonight will be mundane enough to discourage him from his notions."

"They were *my* notions first," I reminded him.

"Yes, well..."

CHAPTER THREE
A Brush With Death
& a Chase

The two ladies arrived at 8:30 that evening, and we made our preparations.

Doyle and I were fine as we were, but Holmes felt the need to don a simple disguise.

"We do not know what or whom we will be dealing with," he said. "As the writer of the note is an unknown quantity to us, so must *we* be to *him*. Miss Morstan, you shall be yourself. I shall be an invisible man. Miss Adler and the two doctors will be our support staff on the scene."

He laid out his plan for us. It was quite simple, and soon we were on our way in a hired carriage.

Miss Morstan was muffled in a dark cloak, and her face was composed but pale. She must have been more than woman if she did not feel some uneasiness at the strange enterprise upon which we were embarking, yet her self-control was commendable, and she readily answered the few additional questions which Sherlock Holmes put to her as we rode to our rendezvous. Miss Adler kept her oar in, making barely-relevant comments and odd observations, earning stern glances from Holmes, which she ignored. Fortunately, the journey was a short one, not much more than three miles. Doctor Doyle and I sat quietly.

The day had been a dreary one, and a dense fog lay low upon the great city. Mud-colored clouds drooped sadly over the muddy streets. Down the Strand the lamps were misty splotches of diffused light which threw a feeble circular glimmer upon the slick pavement. The yellow glare from the shop-windows streamed out into the steamy, vaporous air and threw a murky, shifting radiance across the crowded thoroughfare. There was, to my mind, something eerie and ghostlike in the endless procession of faces which flitted across these narrow bars of light—sad faces and glad, haggard and merry. Like all humankind, they flitted from the gloom into the light and so back into the gloom once more. I am not subject to impressions, but the dull, heavy evening, with the strange business upon which we were engaged, combined to make me nervous and depressed. I could see from Miss Morstan's manner that she was suffering from the same feeling. More than once she pressed a palm to the side of her head and squinted her eyes, as though in pain.

At the Lyceum Theatre the crowds were already thick at the side-entrances. In front a continuous stream of hansoms and four-wheelers were rattling up, discharging their cargoes of shirt-fronted men and be-shawled, be-diamonded women.

Our cab circled the block twice so that Holmes could make observations, then stopped briefly on Wellington Street to let Miss Morstan out at the appointed spot, before continuing on around the corner to travel a short way down Exeter Street, where the rest of us disembarked. Holmes dismissed the driver, then stepped into a dark niche between two buildings and removed his overcoat, which he handed to me. Now clad in a shabby old suit of mismatched clothes, he wandered unsteadily up Exeter Street toward the Lyceum; a poor, unfortunate soul who was no longer quite respectable, but not yet a beggar—one saw his like on the streets of London every day. One or two of the theatergoers might glance at him with pity, then forget him entirely within a few seconds.

Doyle, Miss Adler, and I followed him at a distance. We did our best to pretend to be carefree strollers, out for an enjoyable evening. Though there seemed nothing particularly threatening about our errand, it was still shrouded in mystery, and I had an unaccountably strong sense of imminent danger. In spite of my military service, I consider myself a doctor, not a soldier; however, I had, during my wartime service, developed a sort of "sixth sense," so to speak, and it was worrying at my mind now. Holmes must have had a similar feeling, hence his disguise.

Miss Morstan stood next to the pillar, glancing about. She seemed quite composed, giving no signs of agitation. She might have been waiting there between performances for a friend.

After three or four minutes, we saw a small, dark, brisk man approaching her. I became alert and whispered to Doyle and Miss Adler to take note of the fellow.

He was unsavory-looking—not so much rough as what I will call "slimy" for want of a better term. He had the air of a fellow who wished to appear respectable but lacked the fortitude to achieve such status on his own merits. The suit he wore was no doubt as expensive as it was tasteless. His face was both soft and hard at the same time—lacking in character, callous and ruthless.

"You will excuse me, miss," I heard him say. "This is not personal, I assure you."

Whereupon he produced a small revolver, which he aimed at Miss Morstan's head, point blank. An expression of utter horror blossomed on her pale face. She drew back, but did not scream. Doyle and I were already moving as quickly as we could, but we had little hope of forestalling a tragedy.

We needn't have worried. Holmes, who had been leaning against the wall near the pillar, shaking his head and muttering to himself, sprang forward and disarmed the gun-wielding fellow with a short wooden club.

"There will be none of that, my good fellow," he barked. The ruffian scowled and swung at Holmes with his fist. The detective ducked to avoid it, snatching up the dropped revolver in the same motion.

By now, some of the theatre patrons had become aware of the altercation and were moving away from the combatants with cries of alarm.

As Holmes straightened up, pistol in hand, the would-be assassin dashed to the other side of the street, weaving among the scattering crowd so that my friend could not risk a shot, and jumped into a carriage. The driver, obviously a confederate, wrapped in a cloak with a deerstalker cap pulled down to obscure his face, whipped up the horses and they were off.

Holmes was not to be denied. He bounded over to the nearest hansom cab and instructed the driver to follow the fleeing carriage. The poor fellow started to balk, but his protests died in his mouth as Holmes thrust a handful of banknotes in his direction.

By now, Doyle and I, followed closely by Miss Adler, had reached poor Miss Morstan, who seemed quite done in by her experience.

"Doyle!" Holmes shouted when he caught sight of us, "Look after the women. Watson, with me!"

I barely managed to haul myself into the vehicle as it began to move.

We tore through the streets, around corners, across intersections, until I was quite lost. I believed that we were trending south and west, and must have been somewhere in the vicinity of Belgravia, but I could not be sure.

The carriage increased its lead. Holmes took turns berating our driver and offering him more money, but we were losing ground. Our quarry careened around a corner and we lost sight of it.

"Damn it all!" Holmes cried. "We cannot lose them now!"

But we could, and, as we rounded the corner, we saw that we had.

The carriage stood in the middle of the street, abandoned. There was no sign of the late occupants.

"The carriage was probably stolen," Holmes remarked. "Not *probably*— it most *certainly* was. See here, these gloves certainly belong to a lady who can afford the finer things. No, we will find nothing here to lead us to our quarry. Well, I have his pistol, and perhaps it will tell us something."

"We do have one clue," said I. "By that I mean the area in which the vehicle was abandoned. Those men must have gone to ground somewhere nearby."

"Most likely," Holmes agreed. "Though their destination will surely not be found on this particular street. They are at least that clever. There is no way to trace them now, unless we wish to knock up the inhabitants of every house for a mile around. But we are not empty-handed, my friends. We have a general direction, which is something. The real work will begin upon the morrow. And do not forget, I have one other clue—the fellow's revolver. For now, let us return to Baker Street. We'll drop in at the nearest police station to report our little adventure. Say nothing of the pistol I obtained from our friend."

When we returned to our rooms, we found Doyle and the ladies waiting for us.

"The man who attempted the assault," said Sherlock Holmes, "was not unknown to me. I am certain that he is one Aloysius 'Pigeon' Davies. He is well-known in the London underworld as a man who may be relied upon to perform any task, no matter how unsavory, if his price is met."

"A hired gun," said Doyle.

"Just so," said Homes with a crisp nod. "I might be able to lay my hands upon him within a day or two. Unfortunately, his modus operandi involves a number of intermediaries. He almost never makes direct contact with the party who engages his services."

"So, if he were caught," said Doyle thoughtfully, "and pressure applied..."

"Not only *would* he not reveal the name of his employer," Holmes finished, "he *could* not. And beyond that, he is so devilishly clever that he almost never leaves evidence of his own identity at the scenes of his crimes. To my knowledge, he has been arrested only once during a career that spans almost two decades. He was apprehended in 1877 in connection with a gold robbery. The principals in the crime got away clean, and were never identified. The only bright spot, if one could call it that, is that the miscreants did not profit from their crime—they attempted to flee in a motor launch on the Thames. But the police had been alerted and had a launch of their own at the scene. The thieves were pursued and at one point, the loot went over the side of their launch. The details in the official report are a bit murky. The two men got away, but they were empty-handed. Divers were brought in, but the jewels were never located.

"One other man, apart from Davies, was charged, but it was determined that he had merely acted as a lookout, and he professed ignorance as to the identities of the masterminds. So did Davies, of course, but he was charged as an accomplice, as he had a firearm in his possession.

"However, before he could be brought to trial, the physical evidence that implicated him mysteriously went missing from police headquarters. The authorities had no choice but to set him free. He has been extremely careful since then."

"I imagine so," I said. "But he seems to have abandoned that policy tonight."

"Not necessarily. He was expecting to confront a lone young woman. But I will allow that the scheme was poorly-conceived by someone. Why send Miss Morstan a note which might be found by police? The handwriting would be untraceable, of course, but the authorities would have their suspicions aroused. Why not simply stage a robbery or a burglary or some other situation that might make it look as though the young lady had been murdered impulsively by an impetuous thief?"

"And what of the other man?" I asked. "The driver of the carriage?"

He shook his head. "Again, I lack sufficient data. However, I shall give the matter a great deal of thought, based upon the scant information that I have. Perhaps something will suggest itself."

"The fact that you trailed him to such a fashionable neighborhood seems suggestive," said Doyle. "If the carriage-driver wasn't just running blind, he must have a connection with someone who lives there."

"Yes," said Holmes. "Perhaps he is a step closer to the principal than Davies is. But I would not care to speculate just yet. In the morning, I shall go have a look around the area. You see, Doctor Doyle, the life of a consulting detective is not an unrelieved series of miraculous deductions and thrilling confrontations with dangerous miscreants. Oh, there is a bit of that, as you saw earlier—but it is, in the main, tedium and drudgery; sifting through piles of irrelevant data in hopes of finding a fleck or two of gold."

At this point, Miss Morstan, who still seemed quite shaken by her experience, complained of a terrific headache. Doyle offered to see her home to her quarters at Mrs. Cecil Forrester's house, and administer a sleeping draught. Miss Adler said that she would accompany her friend and remain with her.

When our guests had gone, I pressed Holmes for further information on the pistol he had taken from the attacker.

"Ah, yes, the revolver. Well, it is a Webley, produced within the last three years, I should say. Someone has gone to the trouble of eradicating the serial number. I may be able to bring it out by chemical means, but there's no guarantee of that.

"This is suggestive. As you may or may not know, the London Metropolitan Police have given their officers the option of going armed as a result of the murders of two officers last year. The weapons provided are Webleys like this one."

"Do you think a police officer has done this?"

"Pigeon Davies is hardly a police officer—but someone gave or lent him this pistol. I would like very much to know the identity of the man who drove that carriage."

CHAPTER FOUR
Thaddeus Sholto & Oscar Wilde

he following morning, I found that Holmes had risen and left the house by the time I got myself out of bed. Gazing through the front window at the dark house on the other side of Baker Street, I saw that the weather had not improved at all since the previous night—it was dull and dreary, with low-hanging, dun-colored clouds that threatened rain. As I was sitting down to a late breakfast, my fellow-lodger returned. No sooner had he seated himself at table than the bell rang and Mrs. Hudson showed Miss Adler and Miss Morstan up to our sanctum.

"Well, Mister Holmes, have you made any progress?" Miss Adler demanded without preamble. Miss Morstan said nothing.

"Precious little," Sherlock Holmes answered blandly. "As you can see, I have barely begun work on these eggs, and my toast and coffee are as yet untouched."

"You know what I mean," she said tartly.

"How can I know if you refuse to be specific?"

"Very well, have you made any progress *on Mary's case?*"

"I reported the attack to the police," said Holmes. "They told me there was nothing they could do, just as I expected. They did trouble to investigate the carriage. It had been reported stolen earlier in the evening, and has been restored to its rightful owner. We are not dealing with an amateur here."

"Do you think Mary is in danger?" Miss Adler asked.

"I doubt it," said Holmes. "Whoever was behind that business is now aware that she has friends who will protect her. Still, it would be wise to take precautions."

"Indeed," said Miss Adler, reaching into her large handbag. "Which is why I have this."

She withdrew from her bag a small pistol. "I know how to use it, and I can coach Mary." She handed the weapon to her friend, who looked at it is though it was an artifact from some unknown civilization.

"Oh, Irene, I don't think I..."

"Hush, Mary. I'll feel better if you carry it, and I know you are not heartless enough to cause me undue anxiety. Do you remember that summer we spent on my uncle's farm, when we were girls? You learned to shoot then, and you weren't bad at it. You just need a bit of instruction and practice to refresh your skills."

Mary Morstan sat there and nodded dumbly. The pistol lay in her lap like a dead animal.

"I have one of my own," Miss Adler continued, "and I believe that, between the two of us, we can repel any further attacks."

"That seems to settle it, then," Holmes said. "You are to be commended for your courage and determination, Miss Adler. Just take care not to shoot the postman. And now, on to other matters. I have made a discovery that could conceivably constitute progress.

"I have obtained a list of the names of every house-owner on that street and the surrounding ones. I believe you will find one of the names to be of particular interest, Miss Morstan."

Holmes produced a sheet of paper, handed it to her, and pointed out a particular notation.

"*Sholto*," she read. "Why, that is the surname of my father's friend, the Major."

"Indeed," said Holmes. "Suggestive, is it not? The house, which did in fact belong to your father's friend, is called *Pondicherry*, after the city in India. I have never understood why some people feel the need to name their houses. An address is sufficient. What sort of grandiose appellation could be more apt for these quarters than the very simple *221b Baker Street*?"

"I could think of a few," said Miss Adler. "*Pandemonium* might do nicely, or perhaps *Pompeii After Vesuvius*. However do you manage to find any of your belongings amidst this chaos?"

"He knows exactly where everything is," I offered. "Were someone to slip in and tidy up in his absence, *that* would be chaos."

"At any rate," said Holmes, ignoring Miss Adler's and my remarks, "Major Sholto has passed away, and the house is now owned by his son, Thaddeus."

"Thaddeus Sholto!" Miss Adler exclaimed wonderingly. "Surely not!"

"You know him?" Holmes asked.

"I know *of* him," she replied. "Most people know *of* him; very few *know* him. I knew the name of Mary's father's friend, of course, but I did not make the connection. Thaddeus Sholto is something of a social butterfly, or perhaps a lion, I cannot be certain."

"I never met the major," said Miss Morstan, "or his son. I know nothing of the family. He was Father's friend, I had no dealings with him."

"Then it might interest you to know that Major Sholto died in 1882, on the first of May, just three days before the mysterious advertisement appeared in the newspaper."

"What could it mean?" Miss Morstan wondered.

"There may be no connection," said Holmes, "but it would be wise at this point to proceed as if there were. And if so, why send you pearls for three years running, then suddenly attempt to kill you? Who would do such a thing?"

"It makes no sense."

"There are cross-purposes at work here," Holmes said thoughtfully. "We are dealing with opposing factions of some sort."

Miss Adler had been silent, with a somber expression upon her face. Finally, she spoke:

"If that is indeed the house from which the assassins were dispatched," she said, "I may be able to provide you with some information. As I say, I am not acquainted with Mister Sholto, but I know several people who are. I shall ask around among my theatrical friends, I am sure some of them have attended his famous soirees, and they may have knowledge that you will find useful. I have heard mention of some sort of scandal involving a member of his family, but I have no details."

"If you can send someone my way who *does* have such details, I would be most grateful," Holmes said.

At three o'clock on the afternoon of the following day, we heard the bell at the front door, followed shortly by footfalls on the stairs. With her customary tap upon the door, Mrs. Hudson ushered in one of the most singular visitors ever to grace our humble rooms.

Our visitor immediately made a remarkable impression upon me. It was as though a small crowd of people had entered, rather than just one man. He had a remarkable presence that seemed too large to be confined to a single individual.

He was quite tall and broad. He might have been physically intimidating, but there was an air of gentleness about him. His face was full and his eyes heavy-lidded. He seemed to be perpetually in the process of emerging from a deep, dream-filled sleep, reluctant to return fully to the waking world.

"There are cross-purposes at work here."

His dress was perhaps a bit foppish. To my mind, it strayed a bit beyond the borders of strict good taste, without quite being garish.

"You simply must be Mister Sherlock Holmes," said he. "Irene was quite right, you are a rather formidable-looking specimen. You remind me a bit of the American President Lincoln. Has anyone mentioned that to you before?"

I smiled, as Doyle had made the very same remark to me.

Wilde looked around our cluttered sitting-room. "Irene described your quarters as 'rather Bohemian.' It seems the dear girl has an unexpected genius for understatement."

Wilde had a marvelous speaking voice, and delivered all of his remarks as though he were on a stage. Though he seemed to have taken steps to eradicate it, the faint Irish brogue asserted itself now and again.

"And whom do I have the honor of addressing?" Holmes asked, pronouncing the word "honor" in such a way as to indicate that it was more akin to an unwelcome duty.

Our visitor smiled and sketched a somewhat mocking bow from the waist. "I am a gentleman of whom it is often said that no introduction is necessary, or, perhaps, desirable, but it seems that my fame has not yet permeated every nook and cranny of Baker Street. I am called Wilde, Mister Holmes, Oscar Wilde."

"The name is unfamiliar to me," said Holmes.

"I am a poet, aesthete, and playwright," the man declared, "whose most celebrated works no doubt lie ahead of him. One day you will have heard of me, and you'll realize that you should have been a great deal more impressed than you seem to be at the moment."

In fact, I had heard of Wilde, and was certain that Holmes had as well. Oscar Wilde was far from unknown, even then. Indeed, one would have had to put forth some effort *not* to have been aware of Oscar Wilde. But my friend was prone to feigning ignorance on various topics in order to produce an effect. In this case, it was plainly his intention to knock the brash fellow down a peg or two. He was most adept at that sort of thing, but he would soon learn that, in the irrepressible Wilde, he had met his match.

"Do have a seat, Mister Wilde," Holmes said politely. "This is my friend and associate, Doctor John Watson."

When we were settled in chairs with drinks in our hands, Holmes asked our guest what he knew of Thaddeus Sholto.

"Young Master Sholto is something of a dandy, and a great favorite in certain social circles," Wilde said. "He numbers among his intimate acquaintances a smattering of cabinet ministers, a motley assortment of wealthy dowagers, a dozen or so playwrights, and countless artists of various kinds. Some of his friends are famous, but the true common denominator is money."

"Does he number you among his friends, Mister Wilde?" Holmes asked.

"I do wish you would call me Oscar, Mister Holmes. I would hate to keep a man as fascinating as yourself at arm's length for however long our acquaintance might last."

"Very well," said the detective with a thin smile. "Nor shall I stand on ceremony with you. Do please dispense with the 'Mister' and call me Holmes."

"That is as intimate as he gets, I'm afraid," I offered. Holmes gave me a brief scowl, while Wilde looked delighted.

"Does Mister Sholto have money of his own," Holmes continued, "or does he rely on the members of these social circles for support?"

"Oh, he appears to be at least as rich as Croesus, if the amount of money that flows from his pocket is a reliable indicator. My understanding is that he and his brother found themselves in possession of a veritable mountain of the stuff when their father departed this life."

"I see. And is this brother of his as profligate as Thaddeus?"

"I could not say. He is something of a mystery. I have never laid eyes on Bartholomew, nor has anyone else that I know of. According to Thaddeus, he inhabits the upper reaches of the family home and tends strictly to his own business, whatever that might be. He seems to be completely antisocial, and he may have the right idea. I sometimes think I would be better off in total isolation; that way, I could be certain that everyone with whom I kept company admired me without reservation."

"This Bartholomew sounds a bit like your brother Mycroft," I said to Holmes. I regretted it instantly, and steeled myself for a rebuke. Much to my relief, my friend merely nodded.

"He does indeed, Watson," he said thoughtfully. "And Mycroft has good reason, over and above his natural inclinations, to render himself socially invisible. Perhaps Bartholomew Sholto does too." He was silent for a few moments, then addressed Wilde again.

"You did not answer my question, Mister... ah, *Oscar*."

Wilde laughed. "I ought to have known you'd notice that. The fact is that no true friendship exists between myself and Thaddeus Sholto. I should not be surprised to learn that I wish it were otherwise. I have attended half a dozen of his soirees in the company of mutual comrades, and exchanged perhaps twice that many words with him, none of which were remotely intimate. He may be wary of me for some reason. Perhaps my treacherous reputation has preceded me and whispered a cautionary tale in his ear."

"But you are known to him," said Holmes, "and could plausibly gain entry to his home during one of his entertainments?"

"I believe so, yes. I have not received an invitation recently, but I flatter myself that I do not need one. Sholto holds his little soirees at least three times a week. I can find out when the next one is scheduled."

As it happened, there was to be a 'do' that very night. It was decided that I should accompany Wilde, along with the two ladies and Doctor Doyle, who was eager to involve himself in one of Holmes' investigations.

Holmes used his growing fame as his reason for staying away. His name and likeness had recently appeared in the papers for three straight days in connection with a case—much to his professed annoyance. I had my doubts. On the one hand, he complained bitterly of the notoriety. On the other, he did not refuse a single request for an interview, and seemed irritated when the requests ceased.

I suggested that he employ one of his amazing disguises, but he would have none of that.

"It would be unwise for me to go near that house at present," he said adamantly. "You shall be my eyes and ears, Watson. Observe as much as you can, and bring your observations back to me. The same for the rest of you. I must hold myself in reserve until I have more ammunition in my stores. But, if you have an interest in amazing disguises, I believe I can accommodate you.

"You, my boy, will be the influential, if utterly unknown, literary critic for one of Europe's greatest unspecified newspapers or magazines. You shall go by the name of Mister James Vane, one that I have used before. I can quickly run up a few business-cards with that name printed on them. Or, if you would prefer to be Sir James, my little printing-press can confer a knighthood.

"I believe *Mister* will suffice," I said. "I should like to draw as little attention to myself as possible."

"Excellent thinking, Watson. You may have in you the makings of a spy after all."

CHAPTER FIVE
At Pondicherry House

That evening, a party of four arrived at Pondicherry. The illustrious—or nearly so—Oscar Wilde was accompanied by the celebrated operatic diva, Miss Irene Adler; with them came Mister James Vane, literary critic *extraordinaire*, and his sister, Miss Sibyl Vane. Mary Morstan essayed the role of the latter. Holmes had decided that she ought to be part of our quartet, on the chance that she might see someone or something at Pondicherry that looked familiar to her. Both Holmes and Irene Adler had done considerable work to disguise her facial features and fit her out in a most elegant evening dress. She was quite glamorous, in fact, and bore almost no resemblance to the rather mousy lass who had originally visited our rooms.

Pondicherry Lodge, situated on the edge of the Belgravia neighborhood, stood in its own grounds and was girt round with a very high stone wall. A single narrow iron-clamped door formed the only means of entrance. It seemed a rather forbidding place at first glance.

We were received at the door by a butler in immaculate livery. The interior, I was pleased to note, was well-lighted; heavy curtains over all the windows made this invisible from the outside.

As we entered, it was clear that we would be left to our own devices for the moment. Wilde pointed out our host, Thaddeus Sholto, who stood chatting merrily with a group of finely-dressed men and woman.

He was most striking. Though I was given to understand that he was thirty years old, he seemed much younger. Thaddeus Sholto was certainly wonderfully handsome, with his finely-curved scarlet lips, his frank blue eyes, his crisp gold hair.

"You know," Wilde whispered to me, "there is something in his face that makes one trust him at once. All the candor of youth is there, as well as all youth's passionate purity. One feels that he has kept himself unspotted from the world."

I looked at him again, and saw that Wilde was correct. Thaddeus Sholto seemed so guileless and innocent, I felt as though I were guilty of some unconscionable outrage, coming here under false pretenses as it were.

And as if that were not enough, I realized that I had no idea what I ought to be looking for. It was unlikely that the criminal Davies would be present, and I did not expect to see a man in a deerstalker cap with a scarf wound round his face. I knew Holmes' method, as far as second-hand information was concerned. He would question me minutely, encouraging me to remember details that seemed insignificant.

So I simply wandered about, nodding at people I did not know, and took in everything that I could.

Among the guests, I recognized Lieutenant-Colonel Sir Edmund Henderson, Commissioner of the Metropolitan Police, deep in conversation with Lord Henry Wotton; a certain doe-eyed and weak-chinned member of the Royal Family; and a handful of other famous faces. I was not dazzled by them. For some reason that I could not name, their presence here seemed sinister.

At one point, I saw that Oscar Wilde had engaged our host in conversation. I drew nearer so that I could hear their words.

"Mister Wilde," Sholto was saying, "I am pleased to see you again. I know you have been here before, and I regret not engaging you in conversation. The fact is, I was afraid I might find myself outclassed. They say you are to the art of conversation what daVinci was to painting."

"Well, that is preferable to Whistler, I suppose," Wilde said in that languid manner he had.

"Have you something against Whistler? He has promised to do my portrait one day, whenever he has the time for it."

"Some promises hold very little promise," Wilde said blandly. Catching sight of me, he beckoned for me to join the conversation.

"Here, Mister Sholto, is a very good friend of mine. Do you know Mister James Vane, the celebrated critic?"

"I do not believe I've ever had the pleasure," said Sholto as he shook my hand. "I'm afraid I've never heard the name before."

"Yes, well," said Wilde, "he works for one of those, you know, avant garde and so forth, on the Continent and all that."

"I see." Sholto peered at me curiously with his bright blue eyes. There was indeed something magnetic about him.

"You've a lovely home, Mister Sholto," said I.

"Thank you," he said, closing his eyes and nodding his head. "I live, as you see, with some little atmosphere of elegance around me. I may call myself a patron of the arts. It is my weakness. The landscape is a genuine Corot, and though a connoisseur might perhaps throw a doubt upon that Salvator Rosa, there cannot be the least question about the Bouguereau. I am partial to the modern French school."

"Yes, quite," I replied. "Couldn't agree more."

"James," said Wilde, "I wonder if, between the two of us, we could persuade Mister Sholto to give us a tour of this lovely home."

"I'd be happy to show you around the ground floor," Sholto said. "The upstairs, I'm afraid, is another matter. I do not go up there. I have everything I need down here."

"Oh, we needn't trouble you," I said. "You have other guests to attend to, after all. We shall speak again soon, I hope, Mister Sholto."

Oscar Wilde touched Sholto's arm and nodded, then continued his perambulations about the room. I stood against the wall, casting my eyes all around, trying to preserve details in my memory. I was not looking for anything in particular. I well knew by this time how Holmes operated. He would want facts and observations that I considered trivial.

I was joined by Miss Adler, who handed me a flute of champagne. She sipped from one of her own.

"Quite a crowd here, eh?" she said smartly. "From all walks of life, it seems."

"Above a certain level," I said.

"Well, yes. I've seen a few cabinet ministers and half a dozen artists. And then there is... Oh, goodness, look there!"

I swiveled my head to follow her discreetly-pointing finger, and saw a most unusual individual.

The man could hardly have been less than six feet six inches in height, with the chest and limbs of a Hercules. His dress was rich with a richness which would, in England—which was, of course, where we were—be looked upon as akin to bad taste. Heavy bands of astrakhan were slashed across the sleeves and fronts of his double-breasted coat, while the deep blue cloak which was thrown over his shoulders was lined with flame-colored silk and secured at the neck with a brooch which consisted of a single flaming beryl. Boots which extended halfway up his calves, and which were trimmed at the tops with rich brown fur, completed the impression of barbaric opulence which was suggested by his whole appearance.

Clinging to his arm, almost as an afterthought, was a woman who might have been an actress or an artist's model or the daughter of a prominent greengrocer. She was attractive and well-dressed, but could scarcely compete with her escort's opulence; the poor girl was utterly eclipsed.

The imposing gentleman had approached our host, and was speaking to him in low tones, his head thrust forward in the manner of one who discusses confidential matters.

"That," Miss Adler whispered to me, "if I am not mistaken, which I am not, is no less a personage than Wilhelm Gottsreich Sigismond von Ormstein, Grand Duke of Cassel-Felstein, and hereditary King of Bohemia."

"However did you remember all of that?"

She laughed. "I memorize entire operas, Doctor. I know his highness a little bit. Enough to know what sort of man he is…and what sort he is not."

"Do try to remember," I whispered back, "that I am not a doctor to-night." I tried not to ponder whatever implications Miss Adler's words may have carried.

"Oh, of course. My apologies."

"And do you happen to know the young lady who is with him?"

"I do not know who she *is*, but I know who she *isn't*. That person clinging to his arm is *not* Clotilde Lothman von Saxe-Meningen, second daughter of the King of Scandinavia. Which is significant because that is who the Grand Duke is to marry in just a few days."

The Grand Duke said something to the young lady which seemed to discomfit her; she pressed her lips together, stood erect, disengaged her arm, and walked stiffly away from him. He then resumed his colloquy with Thaddeus Sholto. The nobleman had a fierce scowl on his face, while Sholto was evidently nonplussed by what he was hearing.

Here was something incongruous; just the sort of material that Holmes relished.

I wandered inconspicuously in that direction, not looking at the two men, but moving to within earshot. Finally, I was only a foot or two away, with my back to them. Fortunately, I could see their faces in a looking-glass on the far wall.

"I tell you now, I have no intentions to pay you so much as a pfenning," said the Grand Duke in a low growl.

"I've no idea what you're referring to," said Sholto; he seemed to me to be genuinely perplexed.

"I shall create problems for you," said the nobleman, "such as never be-fore you have dreamed of."

Sholto seemed quite flustered, and appeared to be wilting under the Grand Duke's forceful attention. I felt inclined to go to his rescue, for rea-sons I could not elucidate even to myself, but I resisted. I had the sense that my observations this evening would be of value to Holmes, and was determined to remain an uninterested observer.

Wilde, meanwhile, had made a circuit of the room. Many of the guests knew him personally, and those who did not pretended that they did, as he told me later.

For my part, I meandered about the room, absorbing data about the furniture and fittings; one never knew what Holmes would consider important. I stopped for a moment to peruse the titles on Sholto's large bookshelf. Most of the classical works of literature were represented, along with a few I had never heard of. One volume in particular caught my eye on account of its well-worn condition. It had obviously been consulted more often than any of the other tomes on the shelves. I slid it out and read the title: *À Rebours*, by Joris-Karl Huysmans.

It was in French, of which I possess only a bare smattering, so I could make nothing of the contents. I did notice, however, that the book had been published in May of 1884, making it a less than two years old. Someone in the house must have been very fond of it, I thought, for it to have become so dog-eared in so short a time. I turned to the flyleaf. There was a name inscribed there, in a very peculiar hand, an initial I could not make out, followed by the surname Sholto. It appeared as though whoever had written it had been agitated or perhaps had been writing in an awkward position. Thus, I could not tell if this writing resembled any of the samples Miss Morstan had shown us.

"Interesting reading, James?"

I turned to my "sister."

"I have no idea, *Sibyl*. I have a bit of French, but not nearly enough to make anything of this."

She took the volume from me and thumbed through it.

"Oh my goodness," she said. For the next few minutes she perused the volume, uttering small cries of 'dear me!' and other mild expressions of distress. After a minute or so of this, she shut the book firmly and shoved it back into its niche on the shelf. I noticed that her cheeks had reddened slightly.

"Whatever is the matter?" I asked solicitously.

"It's nothing, I just..." She shook her head. "It's nothing," she repeated.

The hours passed. I talked to people I did not know, heard things I did not understand, and said things that I cannot now recall. (Oscar Wilde later told me that I spoke enthusiastically about the symphonies of William Shakespeare and the comedies of Leonardo daVinci, but I believe he was pulling my leg.)

Wilde seemed quite enamored of our host. I had studied him myself, attempting to apply Holmes' methods to my assessment of his personality. I had never before tried to do such a thing, but I gave it my best effort. I eventually realized that I found him charming in his way, but not terribly appealing. He struck me as rather vapid, in fact. He was dazzling with his good looks and gentle, ingratiating manners, but there seemed to be nothing much beneath it. That was the result of my application of Holmes' methods. Had I relied upon my own impressions and feelings, I realized, my assessment would have been much different. There was something almost mesmerizing about the man, something that made use of his physical attractiveness, but originated elsewhere.

"That is a strange house," said Wilde, after we had taken our leave of Pondicherry and were in our carriage on the way back to Baker Street. "I consider myself admirably free of superstition, but... Oh, I come away from there with the queerest impressions. A feeling of having been observed intently, almost penetratingly, by something, some entity that..." He shook his head. "I cannot put it into words, Doctor. The house itself felt like a coiled spring. There is a great deal more there than meets the eye, or any of the other senses. And at the center of it, our host. He seems all beauty and innocence, but there is danger there. If not in him, all around him. I cannot explain what I am saying to you, nor can I identify the feelings that have brought it all out of me." He sighed deeply and sat back, a curious half-smile on his lips, but a mildly troubled look in his eyes.

"I think I know what you mean," I said. "I do not consider myself an imaginative man, but there seemed to be something in the air of that place. As for Thaddeus Sholto…" I told him of my own impressions, and also the results of my efforts to apply Holmesian logic to our host. I thought briefly of the strange book that had caused Miss Morstan such consternation, but said nothing about it.

"Do you think we accomplished anything by going there?" the young lady asked.

"We cannot know that," I said, "until we have related what we saw and heard—yes, and what we felt as well, I think—to Sherlock Holmes. He will ask you for details, so I hope you have some for him. I took careful note of the layout and furnishings and so forth. He will want to know everything that he can. Things that seem trivial to us may tell him a great deal."

When we got back to Baker Street, the four of us took seats around the sitting-room, while Holmes sat on the floor, legs folded Indian-fashion. He plied us with one question after another, jumping from one to the other of us and back again in a manner that was almost dizzying. He collected data on furniture and food, guests and conversations, and a thousand other things.

Inevitably, the subject came around to the curious book I had discovered on Sholto's shelves. When I mentioned the title, which I barely recalled, Holmes showed keen interest. I could not help noticing that the topic caused Miss Morstan fresh distress, and I did not mention her perusal of the strange tome and the reaction it had elicited. She began pressing her fingers to her temples and making faint grimaces. When a break came in the round-robin questioning, she complained of a headache and said that she must go home.

Wilde offered to escort her, but she told him that if he would but help her find a hansom cab, she could make the journey on her own. Miss Adler wanted to go with her, but she would not hear of it.

"Do stay and talk with Mister Holmes, Irene," she said. "I believe I have told everything that I saw and heard, but you might still have some useful information for him. I shall be fine; I just need to lie down in my own bed, that's all. I'll call on you tomorrow, dear."

Holmes questioned the three of us who remained for another hour and a half. Finally, Wilde and Miss Adler bid us goodnight.

"I cannot see it, Holmes," said I once we were alone. "Do you suppose Thaddeus Sholto has been sending Miss Morstan the pearls? Whyever would he do that and why would he then attempt to kill her?"

"Do not get too far ahead of yourself, Watson. I cannot answer any of that as yet. I can see no connection to the business outside the Lyceum, but something tells me that such a connection *does* exist. This business is more complicated than it seemed at first. If I am to make sense of it, I must know more about Thaddeus Sholto and his late father. When I do, perhaps some of the information you gleaned tonight will fall into a pattern."

CHAPTER SIX
A Scandal &
a Murder in Bohemia

ate upon the following morning, half an hour before our lunch-time, Miss Adler arrived at our door unannounced. Holmes greeted her with a short nod.

"I have not heard from Mary today," she said. "I suppose she was still all in, poor thing."

"I have made certain inquiries this morning," said Holmes. "They have yet to bear any edible fruit."

"I wanted to let you know," said she, "that I have taken it upon myself to give you a bit of assistance. You seemed interested in Doctor Watson's account of the Grand Duke's curious behavior at the Sholto house. I thought that if something peculiar is going on there, it may involve him. It happens that I know him…more that just a little bit, Doctor; I am sorry for my mild subterfuge last evening. When he is in London, he stops at the home of Lord Harry Wotton, a crony of his. I called upon his highness not an hour ago and inquired as to the source of his obvious discomfort. He was morose and tight-lipped and would not tell me anything, but when I mentioned that I number among my acquaintances the celebrated detective Mister Sherlock Holmes, his manner underwent a transformation.

"He asked if you were discreet. I said that you were exceedingly so. I made quite a point of that. I said that you sometimes worked with the police, but that you would never betray the confidence of anyone who came to you for help. He said that he would come.

"He will no doubt attempt to play some sort of a game with you, for such is his nature. What form it might take, I cannot imagine, but I trust that you will not allow him to get away with it. Be firm, but not overbearing."

Homes had been eying her darkly as she delivered herself of this admonition.

"Thank you very much, Miss Adler," said he, "for your sagacious advice on how I ought to handle a potential client. Do please send me a bill for your invaluable services, and I shall pay it promptly."

"There's no need to be that way, Mister Holmes," she said sharply. "I am merely trying to help you. I know the man and you do not."

"Holmes is aware of that," I hastened to say. "But he will have his little joke, you know."

Holmes aimed a venomous look at me, but I met it with one of my own. He quickly saw the sense in my attitude and subsided. It was one of my rare victories over his forceful, not to say domineering, personality, and I felt a bit of foolish pride.

"Quite, Miss Adler," he said placatingly. "My sense of humour has perhaps grown a bit stiff from disuse. My apologies. Your efforts are most appreciated."

"Yes, well," she said, sounding far from placated, "I shall just leave you to it, then. Doctor Watson, it has been a pleasure as always. Mister Holmes, good day to you."

She left in something that was not quite a huff, but tended in that direction.

"A formidable woman, Watson," Holmes remarked when she was gone. "I pity any man who finds himself permanently on her bad side...or her good one."

"You might wish to show her a little more forbearance," I suggested. "She does seem to mean well, and she has been a help so far."

"Oh, I have nothing against her. But she seems to be the very embodiment of some sort of challenge, one to which I feel the need to rise at every turn. It is distracting."

"I can understand that, I suppose," said I. "But, as you have pointed out before, my experience of women—if nothing else—is superior to your own. As an old campaigner, I caution you not to provoke her overmuch. A bit of badinage is fine, but there is a line that it is unwise to cross, and you have come perilously close once or twice."

"I shall trust you to help me mind my boundaries."

"You should not be so flippant, Holmes. Women are a serious matter."

We did not have long to wait for the Grand Duke. Just as we finished our lunch, there was the sharp sound of horses' hoofs and grating wheels against the curb, followed by a sharp pull at the bell. Holmes whistled.

"A pair, by the sound," said he. "Yes," he continued, glancing out of the window. "A nice little brougham and a pair of beauties. A hundred and fifty guineas apiece, I should think, but do not hold me to it."

A slow and heavy step, which had been heard upon the stairs and in the passage, paused immediately outside the door. Then there was a loud and authoritative tap.

"Come in!" said Holmes.

The man who entered was familiar to me, though he had taken pains to alter his appearance. It was, without doubt, the Grand Duke, though today he wore a more sober ensemble, for the most part: a dark suit, utterly without adornment, a plain white shirt and a silken necktie. He carried a broad-brimmed hat in his hand, while he wore across the upper part of his face, extending down past the cheekbones, a black vizard mask, which he had apparently adjusted that very moment, for his hand was still raised to it as he entered. The effect was quite ridiculous, and I barely managed to suppress a laugh as he entered.

"You have been recommended to my employer," said he. "He may wish to engage your services. I have been sent to take care of the preliminary negotiations." He looked from one to the other of us, as if uncertain which to address. It was clear that he did not recognize me.

"Pray take a seat," said Holmes. "This is my friend and colleague, Dr. Watson, who is occasionally good enough to help me in my cases. Whom have I the honor to address?"

"I am the Count Von Kramm, a Bohemian nobleman. I understand that this gentleman, your friend, is a man of honor and discretion, whom I may trust with a matter of the most extreme importance. If not, I should much prefer to communicate with you alone."

"It is both, or none," said Holmes. "You may say before this gentleman anything which you may say to me." The poor fellow did not know that he had already said quite a bit in my presence, and that it had brought him here.

Our visitor shrugged his broad shoulders. "Then I shall begin," said he. "You will excuse this mask. The august person who employs me wishes his agent to be unknown to you, and I may confess at once that the title by which I have just called myself is not exactly my own."

"I was aware of that," said Holmes dryly.

"The circumstances are of great delicacy, and every precaution has to be taken to quench what might grow to be an immense scandal and seriously compromise one of the reigning families of Europe. To speak plainly, the matter implicates the great House of Ormstein, hereditary kings of Bohemia."

"I was also aware of that," murmured Holmes, settling himself down in his armchair and closing his eyes.

Our visitor glanced with some apparent surprise at the languid, lounging figure of the man whom Miss Adler had no doubt depicted to him as the most incisive reasoner and most energetic agent in Europe. Holmes slowly reopened his eyes.

"If *your majesty* would condescend to state his case," he remarked, "I should be better able to advise him."

The man sprang from his chair and paced up and down the room in uncontrollable agitation. Then, with a gesture of desperation, he tore the mask from his face and hurled it upon the ground. "You are right," he cried; "I am the King. Why should I attempt to conceal it?"

"I rather wondered that myself," murmured Holmes. "Your Majesty had not spoken before I was aware that I was addressing Wilhelm Gottsreich Sigismond von Ormstein, Grand Duke of Cassel-Felstein, and hereditary King of Bohemia. Do not be astonished. I have my methods."

I smiled inwardly, knowing that in this case, Holmes' *methods* consisted of information given him by Irene Adler.

"But you can understand," said our strange visitor, sitting down once more and passing his hand over his high white forehead, "you can understand that I am not accustomed to doing such business in my own person. A mutual acquaintance suggested that you might be of help...*very discreet* help. The matter is so delicate that I have come incognito for the purpose of consulting you."

"Then, pray consult," said Holmes, shutting his eyes once more.

"I am about to be married," said our visitor.

"So I have heard," Holmes replied languidly.

"To Clotilde Lothman von Saxe-Meningen, second daughter of the King of Scandinavia. You may know the strict principles of her family. She is herself the very soul of delicacy. A shadow of a doubt as to my conduct would bring the matter to an end. And I now find such a shadow cast over me by a scoundrel named Thaddeus Sholto."

"In what way? What has this Thaddeus Sholto done?"

"Threatened to send a certain photograph to my beloved's family, unless I provide him with a very large sum of money. And he will do it. I know that he will do it."

"I shall need more details," Holmes said.

"He introduced me to a... to a *woman*, sir. Do you see what I mean? Do you understand?"

"I know what a woman is, yes," Holmes said dryly. "I number a few of them among my acquaintances."

"Just so. Well, I am referring to a woman of a *certain type*. Do you comprehend this meaning? I do not have to be indelicate in my language, I trust. Are we not all men of the world? So…I am introduced to such a woman while at one of Sholto's affairs, yes? And what then am I to do? I did what any other man would do. Just having a bit of fun, that is all it was, nothing serious. You are a man, Mister Holmes, you understand these things, is it not so?"

"I'm afraid it is not," Holmes said coldly. "Your definition of a man and mine are quite different, it seems. You have behaved dishonorably, and now you seek to escape the consequences of your own wrongdoing."

"Now, see here, sir…"

"Oh, I *do* see. I see very clearly, *your highness*. Thaddeus Sholto introduced you to this young person. What else did he do? Are you suggesting that he held a pistol to your head and forced you to betray your fiancée? Nothing to say to that? I thought not."

The Grand Duke sat back in his chair, seemingly dumbstruck. Holmes was no respecter of persons, and was not afraid to speak his mind to anyone. As far as my friend was concerned, Wilhelm Gottsreich Sigismond von Ormstein, Grand Duke of Cassel-Felstein, and hereditary King of Bohemia deserved no more consideration than did the humblest streetsweeper, nor did he receive it. To a man accustomed to being deferred to on account of his station, Holmes was a most unpleasant surprise.

And yet, the Grand Duke was in a most unenviable position, and he knew it. His own efforts to resolve his situation satisfactorily had failed. He found himself in the unfamiliar and unwelcome role of supplicant. It angered him, but he realized that it must be endured…up to a point.

"Let us not get off on, how do you say it, the wrong foot. I can understand your personal distaste. But you are a private inquiry agent, yes? This makes you something akin to a lawyer, who must accept his clients as they are, regardless of his own personal scruples."

Holmes chuckled. "Touché, your highness."

"I received a letter and a copy of the photograph. There were elaborate instructions about where and when I should bring the money and so on. I was furious. I could not confide in anyone, but I did not need to. I am hardly a stripling or a weakling, eh? It seemed plain to me who had sent the disgraceful thing, so I went to Sholto's home and confronted him. We were alone upon that occasion. He admitted that he had sent the letter and reiterated his demands. He had the effrontery to tell me that I could disregard the instructions in the letter and pay him in person, in cash, at any time before such and such a date! Well, I of course told him to go to the devil and left him there.

"There it stood for a week. Then I received another letter, almost the same as the first, but more impertinent. There was no mention made of our face-to-face encounter, it was merely a reminder of what he wanted me to do and what he intended to do if I did not comply.

"I returned last night to confront him once again. He denied any knowledge of the thing. Right to my face he told me this lie!"

"He could hardly own up to it in front of other guests," Holmes pointed out.

"If he were a man, he would. I said nothing specific. I merely said that I had considered the matter that stood between us. I threatened him with the police of England and the secret police of my own country. I think this last gave him pause. The expression on his face, you see. I saw fear."

"I should think anyone would be afraid of a threat like that," Holmes remarked, "particularly if it came out of a clear sky from a man of lofty station."

The Grand Duke shook his head. "There is more to it. It is not so straightforward as you may imagine. That house of his, and the man himself...something is not quite right. There is perhaps something of the Devil in it."

"If you would care to compose yourself and begin again," Holmes said, "perhaps we can..."

"No," said the man. His temper was quite mercurial, and he was angry once again. "Coming to you was an error. *Consulting detective*! Pah! You are no better than the official police, *and* you show me this disrespect! Where I am from, this sort of foolishness is not tolerated!"

"Then perhaps your highness would serve himself best by returning there," was Holmes' sharp retort. My friend was a great deal more level-headed than was our guest, but still there were certain things he would not abide.

The Grand Duke glared poisonously at Holmes for half a minute. Then he rose to his feet, turned on his heel, and, without another word, took his leave of us.

"That did not go very well at all, Holmes," I ventured.

"I have no sympathy for his highness, and no wish to involve myself in his affairs. But he believes that Thaddeus Sholto is blackmailing him."

"Why do you say *believes*? You have some doubt?"

"I always have some doubt about everything that has not been confirmed by my own observations."

*"Coming to you was an error. **Consulting detective! Pah!**"*

"If he is telling the truth, Sholto threatened him to his face. He could not have been mistaken about such a thing. That seems definitive."

"That is an interesting word—*seems*. Do you ever think about what it really means, Watson?"

"Well, I can say that there *seems* to be something peculiar going on with Mister Sholto, though how it relates to Miss Morstan, the pearls, and the assassin, I cannot say."

"Nor can I," said my friend. "But I shall."

Holmes fretted and fumed for some time. His attempts to busy himself with a chemical experiment were sad failures. Several times he picked up his violin, only to glare at it as though it had in some manner failed to live up to his expectations, and put it down again. He stalked to the window and glared out at the heavy clouds that still hung low over the great metropolis. When he got out his pistol and expressed his intention to practice his marksmanship upon our wall, I felt compelled to intervene:

"Holmes, it is plain that you are troubled, and your behavior is anything but logical. I will leave you to your own devices up to a point, and that point has been reached. If you are dissatisfied with the outcome of your interview with the Grand Duke, I suggest that you take steps to rectify the situation."

He thought about it for a few moments, and the expression on his face softened.

"Yes, yes," he said at length, "you are quite right. He certainly has more information than he gave us. Perhaps I can extract a bit more of it if I approach him in the right way. Very well, then, I shall swallow my pride, Watson, and apologize to the Grand Duke."

We took a hansom cab. The address Holmes gave the driver was in one of the most exclusive areas of London not so very far from the Sholto House, in fact.

"I know a little more about the Grand Duke and his doings than I let on to Miss Adler," said Holmes. "He is staying, as she said, at the town home of Lord Henry Wotton. The families have been friendly for a great many years, and his highness always stays there when he is in London. I know this because of an inquiry I handled some months ago that involved Wotton. He struck me as a very shady character, Watson, though I discovered nothing specific against him. He certainly keeps questionable company.

"At any rate, as for the Grand Duke, he has connections with our own Royal Family—of course—but one gets the impression that all is not rosy there."

I nodded. "Families can be breeding grounds for ire and resentment. Mine certainly was. And I imagine that royal blood only serves to make it all the more volatile."

"That is most insightful, Watson. You are absolutely correct."

The girl who answered Holmes' knock told us that Lord Henry was not in. Holmes patiently explained that his business was with the Grand Duke. He gave his name, at which point the woman's expression of friendly puzzlement became one of scorn.

"I do not think his highness would care to speak with *you*," she said shortly.

"Shouldn't *he* be the one to make that determination?" Holmes countered. "This might be a very important matter. I have... some fresh information for him, and I wish also to apologize for my boorish behavior earlier. I have nothing to lose, you see, since he is already angry with me. If you turn me away, he might eventually transfer his anger to you, when he learns of it."

The girl found Holmes' argument persuasive. "Very well. I shall give him your name and your message, and then it will be up to him."

She disappeared down the hallway. We heard her tapping on a door. Then the taps became knocks. Finally, there was the opening of a door, followed seconds later by a woman's scream.

Abandoning propriety, Holmes dashed down the hallway. I was close upon his heels.

We found ourselves in what must have been Lord Henry Wotton's library, as most of the walls were covered with heavy bookcases. There, seated before a small table, his upper body slumped over it, was the Grand

Duke. He was absolutely still, and I went to him and touched his wrist. He was quite stiff and the muscles in his face had contracted in a most disturbing manner.

"Dead," I said.

"Send for the police!" Holmes ordered the woman, who stood in the doorway, taut and trembling. She hurried to comply.

"Come, Watson," said he. "Let's have a look before the police get a chance to contaminate any evidence."

He moved around the room, peering at the walls and floors, until he reached the window, where he squatted down and examined the sill. Then he turned his attention to the body.

"Evidence of *what*?" I wanted to know.

"Just put your hand here on this poor fellow's arm, and here on his leg. What do you feel?"

"The muscles are as hard as a board," I answered.

"Quite so. They are in a state of extreme contraction, far exceeding the usual rigor mortis. Coupled with this distortion of the face, this ghastly smile, or *'risus sardonicus,'* as the old writers called it, what conclusion does it suggest to your mind?"

"Death from some powerful vegetable alkaloid," I answered, "some strychnine-like substance which would produce tetanus."

"That was the idea which occurred to me. What then was the means by which the poison entered his system? Here, I think."

He pointed to long dark splinter stuck in the skin just above the ear.

"It looks like a thorn," said I.

"It *is* a thorn. You may pick it out. But be careful, for it is certainly poisoned."

"Shouldn't we leave it where it is until the police arrive?"

"Very likely, but I want to have a look at it."

I took it up between my finger and thumb. It came away from the skin so readily that hardly any mark was left behind. It was long, sharp, and black, with a glazed look near the point as though some gummy substance had dried upon it. The blunt end had been trimmed and rounded off with a knife. I handed the thing to Holmes.

As Holmes was performing his examination, I heard the sound of the front door opening and closing, followed by footfalls in the hallway.

As Holmes quickly but gingerly replaced the thorn in the tiny wound in the Grand Duke's scalp, the footfalls sounded loudly on the passage, and a very stout, portly man in a gray suit strode heavily into the room. This individual was red-faced, burly, and plethoric, with a pair of very small eyes which looked keenly out from between swollen and puffy pouches. He was closely followed by a uniformed constable.

"Here's a business!" he cried in a muffled, husky voice. He turned to the constable. "Here's a pretty business, Jeffers! Who are these chaps? Why, the house seems to be as full as a rabbit-warren!"

"I think you must recollect me, Mr. Athelney Jones," said Holmes quietly.

"Why, of course I do!" he wheezed. "It's Mr. Sherlock Holmes, the theorist. Remember you! I'll never forget how you lectured us all on causes and inferences and effects in the Bishopgate jewel case. It's true you set us on the right track; but you'll own now that it was more by good luck than good guidance."

"It was a piece of very simple reasoning."

"Oh, come, now, come! Never be ashamed to own up."

"Well, at least my *lecture* led you to recover the jewels in that case. It is a pity you didn't have me around when you investigated the Hallward gold robbery in '77."

Jones glared at him angrily for a second, then shook his head.

"What's going on here, then?" he huffed. "Bad business! Bad business! What d'you think the man died of?" He tottered over to the Grand Duke's corpse and performed what seemed to me a rather sloppy visual examination. He gave no sign that he had noticed the thorn.

"Oh, this is hardly a case for me to theorize over," said Holmes dryly, as he watched.

"Then why are you here?" Jones inquired, looking up.

"I came to speak to his highness on a matter of mutual interest. I found him just as you see him."

"I am told, Mister Holmes," said Jones, "that his highness came back here earlier today in a towering rage. Your name was upon his lips."

"Indeed. The Grand Duke and I had a small disagreement. Not quite enough to impel me to murder him."

"I never suggested that," said Jones. "Who says he was murdered at all? Probably had a stroke, he looks the type. But if there is any funny business, I would like to know the nature of your disagreement. I'm sure you can understand why."

"*Post hoc ergo propter hoc*, Jones? That is faulty reasoning."

The inspector responded to this with a blank look.

"Don't try to put me off, Mister Holmes. You can be a rum one at times.

I know you're on the side of the law, but there are those as say you don't mind lying and finagling with the police so that you can solve cases in your own way. I don't hold with that sort of behavior, sir…nor does the Commissioner."

"You may tell Sir Edmund that he has nothing to fear from me. But, as for this stroke theory of yours, you might wish to perform a more thorough *in situ* examination of the deceased. Give your attention to the thorn protruding from his scalp, just there."

At that moment, the conversation was interrupted by the arrival of another member of the detective force.

"Good evening, gentlemen," said Inspector Lestrade. "You're looking well, Mister Holmes. Good to see you, Doctor Watson."

Lestrade was a bumptious little man whose relationship with Holmes was composed of equal parts cordiality and scorn. Though he sometimes mocked my friend, Lestrade actually had a great deal of respect for him, if it was at times a bit grudging.

Lestrade's presence was not appreciated by Jones, as he made quite clear:

"This isn't your case, Lestrade," he said as he plucked out the thorn and stared at it. "It may not be a case at all. Why are you here? Haven't you enough work of your own to keep you busy?"

"Not at present. How did you happen to get this one? A little out of your bailiwick, isn't it?"

"Not at all, Lestrade. I happened to be on hand when the call came in, so here I am. And I don't much like your tone."

"What are you looking at there?" Lestrade asked, pointing at the object Jones held between his thumb and forefinger.

"It is nothing," Jones said petulantly. "Merely a thorn of some sort. It has nothing to do with his death. That's just common sense. It transferred itself to his person from a bush or something, no doubt."

"On the contrary," said Holmes. "No thorn of that type grows anywhere in England. I cannot be precise, but I would surmise that its point of origin is somewhere on the Indian subcontinent, or thereabouts. The same probably holds true of the poison with which it was treated."

Jones glared at him. "Upon what do you base *that* extraordinary statement, eh? If this is some tomfoolery on your part…"

"Not at all," Holmes assured him. "Horticulture is a great interest of mine, and I have produced several monographs on the flora of various regions around the world. I certainly know an English thorn when I see one and also when I do *not*. As for the poison, just look at his face, man! That kind of rictus could not come about as the result of a stroke."

"I believe he's correct, Jones," said Lestrade. "You'd do well to listen to Mister Holmes. He may be unconventional, but he knows whereof he speaks most of the time."

"I don't believe your opinion is needed here," Jones said icily. "I think you have been warned, have you not, about interfering in matters that do not concern you?"

"That isn't what I'm doing, Jones." There seemed to be some hidden meaning in Lestrade's words.

"Perhaps the Commissioner will take a different view. He has done so once already."

"That's my worry, Jones, not yours. Well, if I am not needed, I'll just be on my way then. Good evening to you, gentlemen."

"Lestrade has been disciplined," Jones said after the man had departed, "by the Commissioner himself. I do not know why, exactly…something about a lost firearm, to begin with. He is on thin ice with Scotland Yard, Mister Holmes. And he has recently taken it into his head to shadow and harass me at every opportunity. The situation is becoming an impossible one. But that is not important, Mister Holmes. Did whatever you discussed with the Grand Duke have anything to do with his death?"

"How can I possibly answer that? I do not know who killed him, or why."

"I still do not know that he has been killed."

"You will eventually, Jones. If you've no objections, I should like to have a look around the grounds…particularly the area outside this window."

I noticed then that a small window, partially raised, was situated in the near wall. The Grand Duke, seated at the desk, would have been quite visible from outside. Visible and accessible.

"You may do as you like, Mister Holmes," said Jones. "And I may just join you. Maybe pick up a few invaluable tips, eh?"

"Yes, there are some foot-marks here," Holmes said after he had spent four or five minutes surveying the lawn just outside the small window. "They are not at all helpful, I'm afraid. You see, these here are very small, and whoever made them was barefoot. Just a child at play, no doubt; there are a few of them in the area. In addition to that, there are numerous boot-marks of all kinds…equally worthless. I understand that some tradesmen have been at work. The whole area is contaminated. There is no evidence here."

We left Athelney Jones there, chuckling and speaking about the superiority of common sense over fancy theories.

"I did not know you were a horticulturist, Holmes," said I, as we sat in a hansom cab, on our way back to Baker Street.

"I am not. Nor have I ever penned any monographs on the subject."

I laughed. "Well, I cannot say that Jones didn't have it coming to him. He seems a bit of a buffoon barely competent and overly officious."

"There is that word again, Watson—*seems*. I think there is more to Athelney Jones than there appears at first glance. Just what it is, I am not prepared to say."

CHAPTER SEVEN
The Empty House & Toby

The following day, Miss Morstan called at 221b. She was composed in manner, but the lines around her eyes and tautness about her lips betrayed inner tension. I supposed that she must be one pins and needles over her current situation, and the fact that we were no closer to discovering the secret of the mysterious pearls. My heart went out to her, though there was nothing I could do apart from offering a sympathetic ear.

"Holmes is not in at present," I told her. "And I am not aware of any new developments, I'm sorry to say. I do not know when my friend will be back."

"That's all right," she said. "I'd rather speak with you. Mister Holmes is rather... I don't quite know how to put it."

"I believe I know what you mean. Clients do occasionally find him off-putting. He is an unusual man. He means no harm, and he really is very sensitive. He just... loses track at times. Brilliant men can get away with that, I am told."

"Has he any other clients at present? Anyone... interesting?" She was hesitant, almost fearful, it seemed to me.

"You are worried that he is not giving his full attention to your case," said I. "I can assure you that nothing is further from the truth."

She nodded, then shook her head. "Oh," she said piteously, "it is all so... so... I do not know what..."

"Are you feeling well, Miss Morstan?" I asked. "Is anything troubling you? Apart from the obvious, I mean."

"Well, I... No, everything is all right. I'm just concerned about this business. It is not every day, after all, that one has an attempt made on one's life."

"Quite right," I said sympathetically. "But how is your health? Have you had any more headaches?"

"Actually, no," she said. "I have been free of them for... a little while."

I wondered if she had been prescribed some medication by another physician. I would not presume to be so indelicate as to ask.

"I just wondered if Mister Holmes had discovered anything," she continued. "And we never did discuss his fee. I am not a wealthy woman, but I do have those pearls, and I could..."

"Never mind all that," I said. "One thing you may be certain of is that Holmes will not make any distasteful demands for remuneration. He would not dream of charging you at all before he has solved your problem, and even then he will be most reasonable, I assure you."

"Oh, he is... You are *both* so kind. *So* kind. For you to be so concerned about my health, and..."

She broke off and clapped a hand over her mouth, stifling a sob. I saw that a single tear was making its way down her left cheek.

At that very moment, Holmes came into the room with Doyle at his heels. My new friend had been conducting informal interviews with my fellow-lodger whenever the both of them had the opportunity.

Miss Morstan composed herself and chatted amiably for a few minutes about things I cannot now recall. She did not mention her case or the pearls, which I thought was curious. Fearing that she was being too circumspect for her own good, I raised the subject.

"Have you learned anything new about this business, Holmes?"

"Quite a bit. Whether any of it is worth a tinker's dam has yet to be determined. It is exceedingly difficult, Watson, to make any inquiries at all, discreet or otherwise, about... *certain personages*."

We had earlier agreed not to mention the Grand Duke or his apparent murder in Miss Morstan's presence, fearing that the information might be more than she could bear.

We were interrupted by a tapping at our door. It was Mrs. Hudson with a telegram. Holmes tore it open and made an exclamation of surprise.

"Well, this is indeed a momentous day. It seems that one of our solar planets—and no less a one than Jupiter itself!—has decided to leave its orbit!"

"Whatever are you on about, Holmes?" I asked.

He handed me the telegram:

Must see you over the Grand Duke. Coming at once.
--Mycroft.

The reader may recall Sherlock Holmes' brother Mycroft, who figured prominently in two of the cases Doyle and I brought to the public: "The Greek Interpreter" and "The Bruce-Partington Plans." When Doyle and I set down the former for print, I indicated that it was my first meeting with Mycroft Holmes. If fact, this was not the case. I first encountered him during the course of an investigation Holmes pursued in 1883; a matter much too sensitive ever to see print.

The elder Holmes was something of a puzzle to me. Holmes had initially told me that his brother audited the books in some obscure government office. Later on, he admitted that Mycroft Holmes held a unique position in Her Majesty's government. I have never, to this day, learned what title, if any, Mycroft had. Holmes intimated that his brother had a one-of-a-kind occupation of his own creation. Both of the Holmes brothers, it seemed, were self-made men to the nth degree, unwilling or unable to occupy generic niches established by others. Just as my friend was the world's first consulting detective, Mycroft was the very first of his kind...whatever that was.

Holmes was never forthcoming with details, but knowing that Mycroft's intellect was perhaps superior to that of his brother, I assumed that he was engaged in sensitive and momentous work for the Queen.

Physically, Mycroft was the complete antithesis of his brother. Where Sherlock Holmes was lean and energetic, Mycroft was gross and lethargic. He was a man of fixed habits, and almost never varied his schedule. He was a member of the notorious Diogenes Club, and organization for "the most unclubbable men in London." Members were forbidden to speak to one another. It seemed to me that these men were balanced on the precarious line between misanthropy and outright lunacy.

Not ten minutes after the arrival of the telegram, Mrs. Hudson ushered Mycroft Holmes himself into our rooms. He was taller than Holmes and must have weighed almost twice as much. At first glance, he was imposing without being impressive. But the head perched above this unwieldy frame, so masterful in its brow, so alert in its steel-gray, deep-set eyes, so firm in its lips, and so subtle in its play of expression, suggested reserves of energy and purpose wholly incompatible with the gross body.

After introductions had been made, the elder Holmes struggled out of his overcoat and subsided into an armchair.

"I do not like to be rude to your guests, Sherlock," said he. "But I have come to discuss matters of a very delicate nature."

Taking the hint, Doyle excused himself, offering to see Miss Morstan back to the Forrester home. I started to rise from my chair as well, but Mycroft motioned for me to remain seated.

"I have no objection to your presence, of course, Doctor. You are far more discreet than my brother."

After the door had closed on our departing guests, Mycroft turned his penetrating gray eyes upon his brother and spoke: "What business did you have with the Grand Duke?"

"That is a bit presumptuous of you, brother, don't you think?" Holmes replied calmly. "What sort of a private agent would I be if I casually discussed sensitive subjects regarding my clients with anyone who inquired about them?"

"You were working for him, then?"

"I did not say that."

Mycroft scowled. "I have no patience for your rhetorical games, Sherlock, not today. This is a very grave matter, and I must ask you to conform your conduct accordingly. A foreign nobleman has been assassinated on English soil. That is the sort of thing I and my department take very seriously." I had detected a twinkle of humour in the corner of Holmes' eye during this exchange. It seems he took a bit of joy in baiting his somewhat stuffy older sibling. I had done the same with my own brother, before he was forever lost to me. I found it reassuring to see these hints of common humanity in my often-aloof fellow-lodger.

"I am not investigating his death, as such," Holmes said. "Nor was I investigating anything *for* him, strictly speaking. But it does seem to impinge upon the matter I *am* investigating. When I called on him yesterday, the very last thing I expected to find was his corpse. And that is the absolute truth."

Mycroft nodded ponderously. "We are keeping his death out of the papers, Sherlock. As far as most people know, his highness is merely indisposed. In a day or two, we shall have to allow the news of his death to be released. We have not yet decided how we will handle that."

"Is that the royal *we*, Mycroft?"

"It runs a bit deeper than that."

"I see. What of the police? Have they discovered anything?"

"I spoke with Inspector Athelney Jones, who was good enough to visit me at the Diogenes Club. You know that I maintain a modest suite of private rooms there, and that is where we conducted our interview. The police found a poisoned thorn, as you know. It has proven impossible to trace the thorn itself, of course. As for the poison, we have three chemists working over it at this moment. They have made little progress."

"Is that a euphemism for *none at all*?"

"I strive to sound optimistic."

"The effort is wasted. Tell them it will be rather obscure, possibly some vegetable alkaloid found in the Orient or upon the African continent. I would not rule out India."

Mycroft nodded. "Of course, you know more than you are telling me. We may leave it at that—*for the moment.*

"I impressed upon the inspector the delicacy of the government's position in this case, and he has agreed to release no details to the public press. Some sort of story will have to be given out eventually, of course, but we'd like to leave that until after we have conferred with representatives of the Grand Duke's own government. Jones was most agreeable."

"How do you come to be involved?" said Holmes. "If I may ask."

"The fall of Khartoum in February has placed the Empire and her Egyptian allies in a delicate position with regard to interests in the Sudan. Her Majesty's government has entered into a secret agreement with members of the Grand Duke's government. One of those unofficial treaties which are not intended to become public knowledge. If it comes out that he was murdered by a person or persons unknown while on English soil..."

"Is he that important to these negotiations?" Holmes asked,

"Not at all," Mycroft said dismissively. "He is aware of them, but only just. Between us, the Grand Duke is... *was* a bit of a buffoon. That is not the point. The point is that the political situation in Europe is so delicate and so complex that a seemingly insignificant event can precipitate what one might call a domino effect. The murder of an obscure Grand Duke might set into motion a chain of events that ends with the entire continent at war. There is a web of treaties, bloodlines, gentlemen's agreements, ungentlemanly disagreements, ancient enmities, and…of course…the constant maneuvering for greater power. The German government in particular is looking for any excuse to take aggressive action on any number of potential fronts."

"Mycroft, are you suggesting that…"

"I dare not be more specific, Sherlock," said the elder Holmes sternly. "I have told you exactly as much as I think you need to know, and you'll get nothing more, not a crumb."

"You always were stingy when it came to sharing your treats, Mycroft. It is fortunate for you that I possess a more generous spirit. I have information and I shall share it with you freely, if for no other reason than to shame you. You may want to take a discreet look into the doings of a Mister Thaddeus Sholto. He and the Grand Duke recently had words."

"Thaddeus Sholto," Mycroft repeated.

"Yes. The Grand Duke was a guest in his home the other evening, and the two of them had words. What it was about, I cannot be certain. Possibly something to do with a woman. I was not present myself, you see; I have my information second-hand."

"And why have you taken an interest in this Sholto?"

"That is one of *my* delicate matters. I have been making inquiries on behalf of a client. The young lady who just left here, as it happens. I suppose there's no harm in your knowing about it."

Holmes went on to give his brother an account of our first meeting with Miss Morstan, the mystery of the pearls, and the attempted murder.

"I cannot be sure that Sholto was involved," my friend concluded, "I have no information that would lead me to conclude that he was. As for the Grand Duke, Miss Adler said that he seemed agitated and she recommended that he speak with me about his problem; whatever that might have been. He called on me here yesterday, but before we could get down to cases, there was a bit of a disagreement, and…"

"You insulted him," Mycroft said flatly.

"It was mutual," Holmes replied.

Mycroft shook his great head. "It is fortunate that you never went into the diplomatic corps, Sherlock. You'd have had half of Europe at war with the other half."

"In which case, you would have had plenty of work."

"Sherlock, I have cleaned up enough of your messes to last me a lifetime. You must agree with me that we can do without a repeat of that business you got yourself involved in while you were at Oxford. You might be occupying a prison cell to this very day, had I not stepped in on your behalf."

"I was young and headstrong, Mycroft. Will you never cease to bring that matter up with me whenever you are nettled?"

"Perhaps I will on the day that I die, Sherlock. Perhaps then."

With that, the interview was concluded. Mycroft rose ponderously to his feet and donned his coat. A curt nod served as his good-bye.

"You did not mention the blackmail to your brother," I pointed out after Mycroft had gone.

"I did not," he acknowledged. "And he knows I kept something back. If there is a bit of mystery involved, from Mycroft's point of view, then he will look harder and deeper than he would have had I told him all that I know. Better that he do it himself, in his own way. One cannot give orders to Mycroft Holmes, and requests nettle him and make him recalcitrant. He must be goaded and sometimes gulled. I am one of a very few people who are capable of the former, and the *only* one who can accomplish the latter. I have been doing it since I was in primary school. Even our father couldn't..." His voice trailed off, and an expression of deep sadness, or so it appeared to me, passed briefly across his features.

"Nobody knows Mycroft as I do," he went on. "Not even Mycroft."

"Are you certain that you do not simply want to get to the bottom of it before he can?"

"That may well be a factor," Holmes admitted. "But I do not mind benefiting from any information he might turn up."

"It sounds like a rather serious matter," I said. "Perhaps this is not the time for intellectual games."

"Oh, there is more to it than that, Watson. I am not being capricious, and I do not regard it as a game. There is something about this business; I cannot put my finger on it just yet, but it makes me want to be very careful about who I confide in. And I must keep Miss Morstan's best interests in mind. It is possible that hers do not coincide with those of the government. If Mycroft has a flaw, it is that he sometimes focuses on the interests of queen and country so fiercely that he loses sight of his basic humanity. Miss Morstan may have been innocently caught up in something large and dark, and it could destroy her through no fault of her own. I should not wish to see that happen. Such casualties are acceptable to my brother; I do not find them so."

"She has not been blackmailed," I pointed out.

"Not yet," Holmes said darkly.

"And you *did* tell him about the pearls."

"If Miss Morstan is in the kind of danger I fear she is, it will not come from that quarter. At any rate, don't worry, I shall hear from Mycroft again in a day or two, mark my words. He has probably already set an inquiry in motion with regard to Thaddeus Sholto."

"The two of you are so uncannily alike and so utterly different," I said. "Rather like my poor brother Harry and myself, I suppose. Some qualities we have with us when we emerge from the womb, while others are the product of upbringing and experience and a million other subtle and unknown influences."

"Yes, Watson. That which is inborn will persist. As for the rest, it is too great a mystery for a humble consulting detective to work out. Such speculation is the province of philosophers, not logicians. There is much that cannot be accounted for scientifically, and human behavior falls almost completely within that category. As a deductive reasoner, I am concerned only with what I can be certain a person has done. As for the why of it, I can never be anything more than a theorist. I speak, of course, of motivations deeper than the immediate ones; acquisition of money, elimination of a hated rival, etcetera. What fundamental thing makes a person turn to murder to achieve his ends I can never know."

When Doyle returned, he expressed concern about Miss Morstan, concern that mirrored my own.

"I am worried about her," Doyle confided. "Do you happen to know if she is in the habit of using drugs?"

That certainly got my attention.

"I do not," said I. "But I should like to."

"So would I," said Doyle. "She is behaving strangely, and she has an odd look in her eyes. Perhaps it is merely the strain of recent events."

"Speaking of which," said Holmes, "I have had a thought. If the Grand Duke was murdered because he came to me that would suggest that I am being watched. Or, rather, that *this house* is or was being watched."

He wandered over to the window and pulled back the curtain, peering out.

"The house just opposite this one, which you have no doubt looked at a thousand times, Watson, currently stands empty, and has done for several years. Did you know that Camden House, for so it is called, has acquired a reputation as a haunted place? Ask anyone who has lived here for a few years, and they will tell you all about it. There was a dreadful murder there, or three small children were killed in a fire, or God alone knows what. Rubbish, of course, but very potent just the same.

"Let us just step across the way, gentlemen, and see what we can see."

The three of us quit the sitting-room then and crossed the street, making use of a narrow passageway that took us around to the rear garden of Camden House. Holmes led us to the back door.

"Indeed," he said with a smile and a satisfied nod of the head, "this door has been forced, and rather crudely. Excellent! I made it just difficult enough, it seems. Well, let us just step inside and up to the first floor. We'll have a look at all the windows on the street side of the house. There are three of them, all of which are ideal for observing the front of 221b."

Doyle and I exchanged a glance. I was just as puzzled as he was by Holmes' curious words and actions. We reached the first floor and entered what would have been a spacious sitting-room. Holmes went directly to the windows and examined them one by one. Then he turned his attention to the floor before them, crouching down and examining the floorboards.

"Yes, someone has been here. Someone has been here quite recently, and they spent some time in front of this window." His head switched back and forth, and his gray eyes glinted. "Dear me, this is odd. Two most extraordinary individuals, by the look of things.

"I wish you particularly to notice these footmarks," he said, pointing with a long thin finger. "Do you observe anything noteworthy about them?"

"They belong," I said with astonishment, "to a child."

"So it would appear. And look..! Over here is the mark of a left boot with a broad metal heel. But what of these others?"

I looked in the direction Holmes indicated, and saw a series of round, well-defined discs, running parallel to the boot-marks.

"Those are not foot-marks," said I.

"No. They are something much more valuable to us. It is the impression of a wooden stump. You see how they run parallel to the prints of the left boot."

"A wooden-legged man."

"Quite. And I observed tracks identical to these outside the house where the Grand Duke was slain."

"You said nothing of that," I pointed out.

"Because I did not know what to make of it. There was a chance that the marks I saw had actually been made by some of the locals, or perhaps tradespeople. It might have been made by some gardening implement, though I thought it unlikely. That possibility has just been eliminated."

"It occurs to me, Holmes," said Doyle, "that this house is a positive danger to you."

"More of an attractive nuisance, I think," replied my friend, "with the emphasis upon *attractive*."

"I am not following you," Doyle said, clearly puzzled as was I. "This house, standing empty as it is, makes a perfect place from which anyone who wished you ill could not merely keep watch, but also launch a murderous attack."

"Oh, I am aware of that. I have been aware of it for some time. It is most convenient, really. An irresistible lure for anyone who might wish to keep track of my activities. That is why I came in here months ago and spread a thin layer of creosote on the floors, in front of each window.

"Two years ago, Watson, I performed a small service for a royal personage whose name I prefer not to reveal. It was at the same time, you will recall, that you had gone up to Hampshire to remonstrate with your poor brother, and so I was on my own.

"During the course of that investigation, an enemy used this house as a base from which to spy upon me. A pair of assassins, hired by the author of the bad business, used this very room as a base of operations. I worked it out in time to save not only my own life, but the reputation of a most gracious lady.

"After that, I entered into an arrangement with the owners of Camden House. With financial assistance from the aforementioned gracious lady, I took out a lease on the premises so as to ensure that they remained as they were and are…tenantless.

"As my reputation increased, you see, and I found myself handling matters of greater delicacy, and facing opponents who were both clever and dangerous, I came to realize just how valuable such an arrangement could be. I have done some work on the doors and windows to make them easy to breach. Not *too* easy mind you, not enough to arouse suspicion. One must be subtle when dealing with habitual criminals. They are a wily lot.

"This empty house has served me well more than once, and I do not doubt that it will again. The very best way to snare one's enemies, gentlemen, is to allow them to think they are being clever."

"Capital!" Doyle exclaimed. "Really, I must congratulate you, Holmes. Would I be very far off the mark were I to surmise that some of these tales of hauntings originated with you?"

"Superstition can have its uses, Doctor."

"What is our next move?" I asked.

"Obviously," said Holmes, "I must turn to an investigator who possesses abilities greater than my own. If you gentlemen would care to accompany me to Pinchin Lane, we can engage his services."

"I must be getting back home," said Doyle, "but I will drop around later to find out what you have learned. Do be careful."

Pinchin Lane was a row of shabby, two-storied brick houses in the lower quarter of Lambeth. We had to knock for some time at No. 3 before we could make any impression. At last, however, the face of a rather fierce-looking old man looked out at the upper window.

"Go on, you drunken vagabond," said the man. "If you kick up any more row, I'll open the kennels and let out forty-three dogs upon you."

"I know for a fact," said Holmes, "that you have no more than twenty dogs upon the premises at any given time, Mister Sherman."

"Oh, it's you!" said the man. "Bless me, why didn't you say so, sir? Mr. Sherlock is always welcome. Your friend, too, though I have not had the pleasure. Doctor Watson you say? Glad to know you. I'll just be down in a trice and get the door for you.

"Step in, sirs," said he, once he had thrown open the door. I found myself wondering if the poor man were quite sane. "Keep clear of the badger," he said as we entered, "for he bites. Ah, naughty, naughty; would you take a nip at the gentlemen?" This to a stoat which thrust its wicked head and red eyes between the bars of its cage. "Don't mind that, sir; it's only a slow-worm. It hain't got no fangs, so I gives it the run o' the room, for it keeps the beetles down. What is it that you want, sir? Don't tell me, you need the inestimable services of old Toby!"

"A brilliant deduction," Holmes said wryly. "In certain situations, Toby is a better man than I."

Sherman moved slowly forward among the queer animal family which he had gathered round him. In the uncertain, shadowy light I could see dimly that there were glancing, glimmering eyes peeping down at us from every cranny and corner. Even the rafters above our heads were lined by solemn fowls, which lazily shifted their weight from one leg to the other as our voices disturbed their slumbers.

Toby proved to be an ugly, long-haired, lop-eared creature, half spaniel and half lurcher, brown and white in color, with a very clumsy, waddling gait. It accepted, after some hesitation, a lump of sugar which the old naturalist handed to me, and, having thus sealed an alliance, it followed us to the cab and made no difficulties about accompanying us back to Baker Street and up to the first floor of Camden House.

Holmes took a handkerchief and rubbed it on the floor.

"Toby's olfactory sense is perhaps a million times keener than a human being's, Watson, and I mean that literally. It is most fascinating. To him, the minute aromatic traces leading away from this window are bold and unmistakable signposts that will lead him directly to our quarry. He is especially keen on creosote, God alone knows why.

"Here you are, doggy! Good old Toby! Smell it, Toby, smell it!" He pushed the handkerchief under the dog's nose, while the creature stood with its fluffy legs separated and with a most comical cock to its head, like a connoisseur sniffing the bouquet of a famous vintage. The creature instantly broke into a succession of high, tremulous yelps and, with his nose on the floor and his tail in the air, pattered across the room and down the stairs to the rear door.

Toby never hesitated or swerved but waddled on in his peculiar rolling fashion. Clearly the smell of the creosote rose high above all other contending scents.

Strange dogs sauntered up and stared wonderingly at us as we passed, but our inimitable Toby looked neither to the right nor to the left but trotted onward with his nose to the ground and an occasional eager whine which spoke of a hot scent.

Our course took us south and east for about three miles. We crossed the Thames and continued for a time, before the trail took an abrupt turn back west. We soon found ourselves in Kennington Lane, having borne away through the side streets to the east of the Oval. The men whom we pursued seemed to have taken a curiously zigzag route, probably with the idea of escaping observation. They had never kept to the main road if a parallel side street would serve their turn. At the foot of Kennington Lane they had edged away to the left through Bond Street and Miles Street.

I could see by the gleam in Holmes's eyes that he thought we were nearing the end of our journey.

We moved down towards the riverside, running through Belmont Place and Prince's Street. At the end of Broad Street it ran right down to the water's edge, where there was a small wooden wharf. Toby led us to the

Toby made no difficulties about accompanying us back to Baker Street.

very edge of this and around to the back of a small brick house.

"It would seem that they entered this house," he remarked. "You see, it has a nice new padlock on it. Since it is currently fastened from the outside, they will not be found here."

Several small punts and skiffs were lying about in the water and on the edge of the wharf. We took Toby round to each in turn, but though he sniffed earnestly he made no sign.

Close to the rude landing-stage was another small brick house, with a wooden placard slung out through the second window. "Mordecai Smith" was printed across it in large letters, and, underneath, "Boats to hire by the hour or day." A second inscription above the door informed us that a steam launch was kept, a statement which was confirmed by a great pile of coke upon the jetty.

We were approaching the door of the house, when it opened, and a little curly-headed lad of eight or nine came running out, followed by a stoutish, red-faced woman with a large sponge in her hand.

"You come back and be washed, Jack," she shouted. "Come back, you young imp."

"Dear little chap!" said Holmes in an almost fawning manner. "What a rosy-cheeked young rascal! Now, Jack, is there anything you would like?"

The youth pondered for a moment.

"I'd like a shillin'," said he.

"Nothing you would like better?"

"I'd like *two* shillin' better," the prodigy answered after some thought.

"Here you are, then! Catch! A fine child, Mrs. Smith!"

"Lor' bless you, sir, he is that, and forward. He gets almost too much for me to manage, 'specially when my man is away days at a time."

"Away, is he?" said Holmes in a disappointed voice. "I am sorry for that, for I wanted to speak to Mr. Smith."

"He's been away since yesterday mornin', sir."

"I wanted to hire his steam launch."

"Why, bless you, sir, it is in the steam launch that he has gone."

Holmes frowned and nodded his head. Then his expression abruptly brightened. "What about that small house across the way? I was told that a boat captain lived there. Might he be in?"

"That house has been unoccupied for some time, though there have been some comings and goings of late. Not a boatman, though, of that I am certain. I've only had a look at the fellow once, myself, though our Jack has seen him a time or two."

"Is it a wooden-legged man?" said Holmes.

"Not at all, sir. He has two good legs. It was just a day or two ago I seen him going 'round the back. It was funny about him. He was very sort of delicate-looking, if you take my meaning. Sort of soft-like. I hate to put it this way, but it was more like he was *pretty*, as a girl is, rather than handsome like a man would be."

"I see," Holmes said.

"Yes, sir, but that's not the funny thing I meant. The funny thing was the look on his face. It didn't fit in with the way he *looked*, if you see what I'm getting at. I've seen the same expression, the same hard eyes, on men who live in or pass through this area that would just as soon skin you alive as look at you. I know the kind to steer clear of, sir, and this pretty-faced fellow was one I'd give a wide berth to."

"Describe him in a bit more detail, if you would," said Holmes. "I may know the chap. If he is who I suspect, he may be of some assistance to me."

The woman proceeded to give us an excellent verbal likeness of Thaddeus Sholto.

"Did he go through the window?" Holmes asked. I thought it a strange question.

"Oh, no, sir, he had his own key. If I'd seen someone breaking in, I'd have called for an officer."

"And you've only seen him the once?"

"Just the once...and that was once too often."

"Well, Mrs. Smith, as they say, *there's nowt so queer as folk.*"

"That is the truth, sir. Makes me fearful about young Jack, you know."

"I understand. I am sorry, Mrs. Smith, that I did not find your husband in, for I wanted a steam launch, and I have heard good reports of the... Let me see, *what* is her name?"

"The *Aurora*, sir."

"Yes, of course! Well, perhaps another time, for I do a great deal of business, and have heard very good things about your Mister Smith as well as his boat."

The woman beamed at him. "Just drop by whenever you like, sir. If you find him here, you'll not be sorry you engaged him."

"Good-morning, Mrs. Smith. There is a boatman here with a wherry, Watson. We shall take it and cross the river."

"The main thing with people of that sort," said Holmes as we sat in the sheets of the wherry, the dog Toby stretched upon the deck at our feet, "is never to let them think that their information can be of the slightest importance to you. If you do they will instantly shut up like an oyster. If you listen to them under protest, as it were, you are very likely to get what you want."

"I suppose you're right. Seems a shame to mislead her, though. She was such a nice woman."

"The world is full of nice people," Holmes observed. "One must take it as it is. And insincere kindness is preferable to sincere meanness."

CHAPTER EIGHT
A Scandal for Oscar

We took Toby back to his curious home, and returned to Baker Street. We had not been back for half an hour when we heard the downstairs bell, and a few moments later, Mrs. Hudson escorted Oscar Wilde up to our sitting room.

"I received this today," said he, handing a folded sheet of paper to Holmes. "By ordinary post. I was rather disappointed. A thing like this should have materialized in the dead of night, affixed to my front door with a blood-stained dagger."

"Alas," said Holmes, "the world is a largely unromantic place, with occasional flashes of inspired brutality."

"I suppose it will have to do until something better comes along. As for this communication, I found it most interesting in light of what you told me about the Grand Duke."

Holmes unfolded the paper and read what was written upon it.

His eyebrows went up three different times during his brief perusal. If I was expecting him to pass the missive on to me, as he often did with correspondence related to a case, I was to be disappointed.

He looked Wilde in the eye and said, "Are these allegations true?"

Wilde shrugged. "Does it matter? He says he has proof. Any man with the nerve to write such a letter would have no trouble producing proof of anything, whether it was true or not."

"That does not answer my question."

"I realize that."

"What do you plan to do?"

"I have no plans. I had hoped that you might have some suggestions. The sum this individual demands in return for this 'proof' is quite beyond my means. I fear I have done rather too good a job of appearing more affluent than I actually am. Fame and wealth are not necessarily mutually inclusive. I suppose I am fortunate in that some poor souls must make do with neither."

"You have no idea who sent it?"

"I have a suspicion. I suspect you do as well."

Holmes frowned. "Hm." He studied the letter again. "The writer is certainly male, and not without considerable means, if the ink and paper are any indication. It bears, if I am not mistaken, a certain resemblance to the writing on Miss Morstan's letter."

He turned it over and studied the back for a time. "It is, of course, unsigned, but its arrival at this particular time is suggestive."

"I rather thought so. I do not assume that it was sent from the Sholto house, but..."

"Quite right," Holmes said crisply, "One should never assume anything. However, we may take it as a working hypothesis and devise a way to test it. I must gain entry to those premises. Do you plan to return there in the near future?"

"I have no plans at all. If you wish me to, I'm certain I can manage it. If the doctor is willing to once more essay the role of..."

"No," Holmes interrupted. "I must see this man in the flesh and I must gain entry to his house myself. I shall accompany you, Oscar."

"I assume you'll be using one of your clever disguises."

"You assume incorrectly. The time for subterfuge is over. I shall present myself to him as Mister Sherlock Holmes."

"Throwing down the gauntlet, eh?" Wilde asked, humor and excitement dancing in his eyes.

"Merely putting the household on notice," my friend replied. "I do not wish to grapple with anyone just yet. I shall not be calling on him as a consulting detective; rather, I shall let one of my other talents serve as my passport."

This was a most intriguing remark, and Holmes, of course, refused to elaborate. I knew that he was an accomplished violinist, and theorized that his musical ability would serve him as *bona fides* in the rarified atmosphere of the Sholto household.

That settled, Holmes returned to the original topic.

"I must know if there is a possibility that he has any genuine evidence in his possession, Oscar."

When Wilde spoke, he held his head up, looked Holmes in the eye, and did not hesitate:

"The allegations are not false."

Holmes nodded.

"I do not know what evidence he could possibly have," Wilde went on, "but fellows of this kind are devilishly crafty. I have friends who have fallen prey to blackmailers. They obtain documents and photographs as if by magic, and what they cannot find, they can manufacture. Were I to allow him to make his information public. I might find myself in an uncomfortable position. I may feel the need to sue him for slander."

"No," said Holmes. "He will not place himself in a position where he can be sued. The information will be given anonymously to some news agency. You could bring an action against whoever published it, but I fear such a course would inevitably be disastrous for you. There is only one acceptable outcome: Sholto will not give the information to anyone, and it will never become public knowledge. We shall lay our hands on it. That must be our only goal, Oscar, and we cannot settle for anything less. Sholto will be arrested, but before that happens, whatever evidence he has in his possession will be destroyed. Once he is exposed as a blackmailer, one or two of his earlier victims will surely come forward to give evidence against him. Perhaps one of those poor devils whose lives were ruined by him. I will make it my life's work, if necessary, to see to it that they get their opportunity."

When Wilde had gone, I asked Holmes about the nature of the blackmail threat.

"It is one of those things," said he, "that polite people never speak of, though it may consume their thoughts from time to time. When it is discussed at all, it is usually referred to as the 'Sin of Sodom,' I believe."

I was shocked. "You mean... You mean, Oscar Wilde..?"

He nodded. "Apparently so. If proof of the allegations is made public, he could have quite a rough time of it. Completely undeserved, in my view, but things are what they are."

"Do you mean to say that you approve?" I asked him.

Holmes shrugged his shoulders. "It is not for me to approve or disapprove, Watson. And, while it is not my cup of tea, I have never been able to see any harm in it, so long as the proceedings involve consenting persons of legal age. I prefer to save my indignation for things that have earned it. I have yet to hear a truly persuasive argument against the so-called sin, and I do not expect that I ever will. Those who rail against it must perforce take refuge in threadbare tautology: It is evil because it is evil. Bah! Pointless morality, my dear Watson, is nothing more than self-imposed tyranny, and it is absolutely destructive to the logical faculty."

"I believe a prohibition against it may be found somewhere in the Bible, Holmes."

"Ah! That explains why I have never heard of it."

I smiled ruefully and shook my head. I knew that Holmes was quite familiar with the Scriptures, but, as I have mentioned elsewhere, he often feigned ignorance of one topic or another in order to illustrate a point. My friend's tendency to treat both the sacred and the profane in the same cavalier fashion made me a bit uncomfortable at times. While I am nobody's idea of a religious man, I have not discarded the last vestiges of the faith that was drilled into me as a child. I have been known to cling to it, albeit rather feebly, in times of trouble; I must confess, though, that when the sailing is smooth, I seldom spare it a thought. But there are always other considerations, and mine were rather more practical.

"It is a crime," Holmes said, "but there are no real victims."

"Are you certain of that?" was my retort. "Wilde is married and has a small son. Were his proclivities to become known, you might find your victims there. Were he a single man, I might share your attitude; but under the circumstances, it is insupportable."

And there our discussion came to an end.

That evening, both Wilde and Miss Adler arrived at 221b. I knew that Holmes had sent a telegram to the latter that afternoon.

"Oscar," said Holmes, "I believe the best course at present is for you to pay the money."

"But I do not have it."

"I do," said Miss Adler. "And I am prepared to allow you to use it. Mister Holmes and I have discussed the matter, and have come to an agreement.

If things go well, I will get it back. If they do not, I will survive."

"Not to tell you your business, Holmes," said Wilde, "but once a victim shows a willingness to pay, is it not customary for the blackmailer to make further demands?"

"Not always. Those who wish to make a career of it are careful not to overtax their 'clients.' They must maintain a certain reputation, after all. Word of mouth, Oscar. They rely upon it as do many small businessmen. Either way, our aim here is to render the blackmailer incapable of any future endeavors."

Oscar Wilde replied to the blackmail letter by sending a card to a post-office box in a small hamlet outside of London. I suggested keeping watch upon the post-office, but Holmes dismissed the notion. A day later, Wilde received a further communication from the blackmailer, instructing him to bring the money to a certain street corner at a certain time.

"Criminals," Holmes remarked, "should thank their lucky stars for the efficiency of the British postal system."

Finally there came the hour, and we were about to embark on our dark errand. Doyle had arrived and was discussing the situation with Holmes, taking copious notes. Oscar had arrived shortly after, and attempted to engage me in light conversation, but I was in no mood for it.

As we were preparing to leave, a telegram arrived for Holmes.

"It is from Lestrade," he said. "He claims to have information for me, and wants me to meet him at his office as soon as possible. Hm. Very well, then, I shall play the game for now. Watson, if this is what I believe it to be, I already know what I wished to learn. You and Oscar will have to go it alone. I have every confidence in you."

"I shall be glad to accompany them as well," said Doyle.

"Stout fellow," said Holmes, clapping him on the shoulder. I was encouraged by my friend's warming attitude toward Doyle. I was also pleased that I would not be left alone with Oscar Wilde. I saw nothing to be gained by speaking my mind to him, and wished to avoid the subject, and the man, altogether.

The section of town to which we had been directed was an insalubrious one. We were in the East End, somewhere close to Whitechapel. Here, people roamed the poorly-lit streets at all hours. We saw a few figures moving about, some of them wraith-like, some disconcertingly solid and dangerous-looking. Workers going to or from their labors, perhaps in the slaughterhouses nearby; vagabonds; women of dubious occupation; ragged children; all of them so accustomed to poverty and degradation that they saw it as the norm and aspired to nothing more. This was a district in which life was lived from one hour to the next, with no greater future in sight. Wilde once said, "We are all in the gutter, but some of us are looking at the stars." But tonight, we were in a place where the gutter was all there was, and its inhabitants looked at nothing save the gloom before them.

We arrived on the street, a block away from the appointed spot. Doyle and I concealed ourselves between two sad, shabby buildings as Wilde continued on to the corner, one of the few in the area which was illuminated by a working gas-light. He stood glancing nervously about, and I did not blame him. Though he was attired in drab, shabby clothing, he had a great deal of money on his person. He must have been wondering if some of the predators that dwelt in this gutter could sniff it out, in the way that the dog Toby detected creosote.

We did not have long to wait. Scarcely half a minute had passed before a dark figure emerged from the shadows between two dingy brick buildings on the other side of the narrow thoroughfare and slowly approached the spot where Wilde stood. I reached into my jacket pocket and withdrew my revolver, hoping that I would not have need of it.

When the newcomer reached the feeble circle of light, I saw that he was clad in dark trousers, an overcoat, an Inverness cape, and a deerstalker cap. All of his face, but for the eyes, was hidden behind a scarf. He moved a bit stiffly, but I could not say whether or not he had a wooden leg.

He stopped in front of Wilde. A few words were exchanged, but I could not hear them. Wilde reached into his jacket and produced the large brown envelope containing Irene Adler's money. After another brief conversation, inaudible from where I crouched, he handed the envelope to the man in the deerstalker, who turned on his heel and went back the way he had come, disappearing again into the blackness between the two buildings.

"That went rather smoothly after all," said Doyle as Wilde rejoined us.

"I don't know about that," said Wilde, "but as it did not end with me bleeding to death in the street, I suppose it is acceptable. I wonder just what we have accomplished, apart from separating poor Irene from some of her money."

"There was some purpose in it, I am sure," said I. "With Holmes, there always is."

"Spoken like a true acolyte," Wilde remarked.

Upon our return to Baker Street, we found Holmes waiting for us. In fact, he had arrived only a few minutes before we did. I gave him an account of our own rather mundane experiences, and then inquired about his meeting with Lestrade.

"He knew nothing of the telegram," said my friend, "and expressed ignorance and indignation in equal measure, of course."

"Do you believe him?"

"I do. Lestrade is not a particularly clever man, but he is honest; on that I would stake my own reputation, such as it is. We had a nice little chat about some very interesting subjects."

"What the devil is going on?"

"Oh, it is rather obvious to me. To be honest, I expected some such thing but proving it is another matter. I shall make it my business to obtain such proof, but it may not prove an easy task and the clock is ticking. That is why I decided to play the game their way for the moment. Had I not, the man in the deerstalker might not have appeared. We have accomplished something there, at any rate, though I would like to have seen the man for myself."

"What have we accomplished?" I asked, genuinely bewildered.

"We shall see, Watson, we shall see. In the meantime, I believe it is time that I had a firsthand look at Pondicherry, as I mentioned the other day. You have said, Oscar, that Thaddeus Sholto had hopes of James McNeill Whistler doing a portrait of him. Do you think it likely that this will happen in the near future?"

"Not at all," Wilde said airily. "Whistler will promise anything to anyone who seems interesting, particularly if I too am interested in the interesting person. I happen to know that he has made more commitments than he can possibly meet, and that he must perforce assign them to a hierarchy. By any standard he might apply, Thaddeus Sholto would be very close to the bottom, no matter what he might tell the poor fellow."

"Then Sholto is eager, not to say desperate, for the services of a portraitist."

"That, I think, would be a true statement."

"Well, then, I have just the fellow for him. A competent but unknown painter of discernible if not extravagant talent. He has French ancestors who were known and respected in the art world."

"To whom do you refer?" I asked. "Have I heard of him?"

"I daresay you have," Holmes said with an impish smile. "You share breakfast with him most mornings."

"You?"

He nodded his head.

"My dear Holmes," said I, "I had no idea that you numbered painting among your many talents."

"I rarely indulge. Music is more stimulating to me. But my ancestors on my mother's side were artists; my grandmother's brother was Émile Jean-Horace Vernet, whose name may be familiar to you. I have heard his style described as 'archaic,' but that's as may be. He was reputed to be an incredibly swift painter, and I have inherited at least that much."

"I had no idea!" said I, in amazement.

"Something in my blood compels me every now and again to take up a pencil or a brush," he said. "I would not call myself accomplished, but I am quite passable, I think. It is a shame to squander an inheritance of any kind. I do not wish such artistic talent as I may possess to become atrophied, Watson. It does come in handy in the detective trade, you know."

"Remarkably so in this case," Wilde observed.

"I would not have anticipated it," Holmes. "But one must always be prepared to use whatever ammunition one possesses."

"Holmes," I ventured, "do you think this is wise? Won't he know why you have come to him?"

"It can do no harm. As one who has taken the Hippocratic Oath, Watson, you must appreciate that. If he is innocent of any wrongdoing, he will have no reason to suspect me of anything. If he is guilty, he will not dare refuse, and my appearance might rattle him and lead him to commit an error. Or, I might even draw out his mysterious brother. A man will put up with much from someone who is immortalizing him, after all. It seems quite the best course of action."

"There is that word again, Holmes," said I.

"Which one?"

"*Seems.*"

CHAPTER NINE
Holmes Accepts a Commission

olmes and Wilde attended the next soiree that Thaddeus Sholto held. I did not accompany them upon this occasion, nor did any of our other new friends. Things apparently went quite well; Sholto was pleased that the well-known consulting detective wished to paint his portrait. Sessions were arranged, and Holmes set out for Pondicherry for three days running, taking with him his paints, easel and canvas.

When Holmes returned one the afternoon of the third day, he was agitated and preoccupied. He placed his wooden easel and the large covered canvas against the wall and waved a yellow telegram form at me.

"I have unsettling news, Watson. There has been a fire at the Diogenes Club!"

"Good Lord! Was anyone hurt?"

He shook his head. "No. I have been assured of *that*, but nothing else. I have just had a telegram from Mycroft; I just met the boy downstairs, as I returned. He does not say how the fire was set, or even when it happened, but it must have been very recently. He says it was rather minor after all, and that I was not to worry on his account."

"I saw nothing in today's newspaper."

"Nor will you in tomorrow's. If it happened at the Diogenes Club, and Mycroft was involved, it will be treated in the same manner as the Grand Duke's murder. I wouldn't have known of it at all if not for this telegram. Mycroft must hold me in a certain awe if he felt compelled to inform me of something nobody is intended to know about. Perhaps he suspects me of clairvoyance."

"Well, at least he is all right."

"Is he? I wonder. He says he will be 'unavailable' for the next few days, and offers no further explanation."

"Do you suppose he was injured?"

"Perhaps not physically, Watson. If this is what I think it must be; Mycroft was nowhere near the club when the fire broke out."

"Have you any intention of explaining that remark to me?"

"You know my methods, Watson. I will not advance a theory until I am certain I stand upon firm ground. The matter grows both clearer and more muddy at once."

I pondered that remark and got nowhere.

"Well," Holmes went on, "Mycroft will not be approachable at the moment, so I must have faith that he will endure. He always does."

"If you intend to keep me in the dark about most of what is going on," said I, "do at least let me have a look at your work."

Holmes uncovered the canvas and held it up for me to see.

"That is quite a good likeness of Thaddeus Sholto," said I, and indeed it was. Holmes was a more talented painter than he had suggested earlier. As I studied the nearly completed painting, something struck me.

"He looks a bit... *sinister*, though," I said.

"Do you think so?" Holmes stepped back and examined his work with a critical eye.

"Perhaps," he said. "Most curious. It was unintentional, but... Mayhap my current mood has influenced me. Or..."

"Or what?"

"Ask me later. Perhaps I will have an answer at some point. It will require a great deal of thought and reflection. This case is leading me down strange corridors, Watson."

With this curious remark, Holmes made it clear that the subject was closed for the time being, and he refused my requests for clarification. As it seemed to have no bearing on the mystery in which we were embroiled, I thought it best not to pursue it any further.

"Bartholomew Sholto remains elusive," he said at length. "One might almost believe that he did not exist at all. I had ample opportunity to look around on the ground floor of Pondicherry. I noticed unmistakable signs that certain wall panels and other fixtures have been removed and then replaced. Someone has been searching for something. I suspect that Thaddeus has taken the place nearly apart. I was unable to gain entry to the upper stories. The mysterious Bartholomew has secured his little domain against intrusion. At the top of the main stairway, he has installed a sort of fence, Watson. A lattice of thick metal with a door set into it secured on the other side with a heavy padlock."

Holmes and I had an early supper, provided by Mrs. Hudson, and were just finishing up when Miss Morstan made an appearance. She apologized for descending upon us unannounced, and said that she had come up with an idea that she wanted to place before Holmes for his consideration.

"I should be grateful for a fresh viewpoint," said Holmes. I was pleasantly surprised by his attitude. "Something strange is going on in that household. Someone wishes to obstruct our efforts, and will go to great lengths to accomplish it. I have focused my attention on Thaddeus Sholto, but he may not be the one who bears watching. He has a brother, one with a criminal past and a mysterious present. I have observed a great deal, but none of it adds up to anything useful. I have yet to catch so much as a glimpse of Bartholomew Sholto."

"Perhaps we should simply go and ask him," said Miss Morstan. "*Thaddeus* Sholto, I mean. That is my idea. Confront him with what we know, and ask him to tell us whatever *he* might know."

I had not told her of the deaths that seemed to have a connection to the Sholto household. Had she been aware of them, she might not have been so quick to suggest such an expedition.

"Actually," said Holmes, "if I think about it, I suppose I agree with you. Intrigue is what I have spent a lifetime training myself for. Perhaps I have become too accustomed to lies and obfuscation. I do not wish to turn into my brother Mycroft.

"Therefore, Miss Morstan, with that standard applied, your suggestion is a most excellent one."

CHAPTER TEN
Thaddeus Tells His Tale

And so we set out once again for Pondicherry House. Upon this occasion, the Vane siblings were left in the makeup-kit. I was John Watson and Mary Morstan was Mary Morstan. I was sure Sholto would not recognize in her my vivacious "sister," Sibyl Vane. We made stops along the way to collect both Oscar Wilde and Doctor Doyle. Holmes had advanced the theory that their presence might be helpful, though he did not say to whom, or in what way. Both of the men had offered to make themselves available at any time and for any reason, for the duration of this puzzling case.

Thaddeus Sholto himself opened the door for us when we knocked. None of his servants was anywhere to be seen. He seemed surprised to se us, though not put out.

"Mister Holmes," said he, "this is an unexpected pleasure! I don't suppose you've come about the portrait?"

"Indeed not," Holmes said. "I am afraid I'm here in a professional capacity. I hope you will forgive me for my little deception. I have taken some liberties with the truth, but I assure you that the portrait is quite real, and I have every intention of completing it."

"It is really quite good," said Miss Morstan. "I have seen it."

"Yes, Mister Holmes, I did wonder a bit at your offer to do my likeness. I've heard of you, of course. You could very well have just been one of Oscar Wilde's artistic friends. But I suspected that it might have something to do with Bartholomew. He is, I fear, beyond any sort of redemption. I did not know that you knew Miss Morstan here, but I cannot say I am surprised, in light of recent events. If you would tell me what impelled her to seek your counsel, it would be appreciated. Has he done something against you, Miss Morstan?"

"We believe that he, or someone in his employ, attempted to kill her," said Holmes.

"Oh my goodness. Please tell me all about it."

Holmes gave him a concise account of the pearl business.

"I suppose that the cat has most definitively left the bag," said Sholto when he had heard the tale. "I might as well tell you all that I know. Perhaps I can do you justice, whatever Brother Bartholomew may say or do. If he is up to his tricks, I hope we can settle it privately; if he has not gone too far. There is nothing more unaesthetic than a policeman."

"Oh, I don't know about that," said Wilde. He seemed about to deliver himself of an oration, possibly one of his diatribes against some rival of his; Holmes silenced him with a stern glance.

"You will excuse me, Mr. Sholto," said Miss Morstan, "but I am here to learn something from you, if I can. I should desire the interview to be as short as possible."

"At the best it must take some time," he answered. "I must tell you that there are several points in the story of which I am myself ignorant. I can only lay the facts before you as far as I know them myself.

"My father was, as you certainly know, Major John Sholto, once of the Indian Army. He retired some years ago and came to live in this house. He had prospered in India and brought back with him a considerable sum of money, a large collection of valuable curiosities, and a staff of native servants. With these advantages he bought himself a house, and lived in great luxury. My brother Bartholomew and I were the only children.

"I very well remember the sensation which was caused by the disappearance of Captain Morstan. We read the details in the papers, and knowing that he had been a friend of our father's we discussed the case freely in his presence. He used to join in our speculations as to what could have happened. Never for an instant did we suspect that he had the whole secret hidden in his own breast, that of all men he alone knew the fate of Arthur Morstan.

"We did know, however, that some mystery, some positive danger, overhung our father. He was very fearful of going out alone, and he always employed two prize-fighters to act as porters at Pondicherry. Our father would never tell us what it was he feared, but he had a marked aversion to men with wooden legs."

Holmes and I exchanged a brief glance.

"My brother and I used to think this a mere whim of my father's, but events have since led us to change our opinion.

"Early in 1882 my father received a letter from India which was a great shock to him. He nearly fainted at the breakfast-table when he opened it, and from that day he sickened to his death. What was in the letter we could never discover, but I could see as he held it that it was short and written in a scrawling hand. He had suffered for years from an enlarged spleen, but he now became rapidly worse, and towards the end of April we were informed that he was beyond all hope, and that he wished to make a last communication to us.

"When we entered his room he was propped up with pillows and breathing heavily. He besought us to lock the door and to come upon either side of the bed. Then grasping our hands he made a remarkable statement to us in a voice which was broken as much by emotion as by pain. I shall try and give it to you in his own very words.

" 'I have only one thing,' he said, 'which weighs upon my mind at this supreme moment. It is my treatment of poor Morstan's orphan. The cursed greed which has been my besetting sin through life has withheld from her the treasure, half at least of which should have been hers. And yet I have made no use of it myself, so blind and foolish a thing is avarice. The mere feeling of possession has been so dear to me that I could not bear to share it with another. See that chaplet tipped with pearls beside the quinine-bottle. Even that I could not bear to part with. You, my sons, will give her a fair share of the Agra treasure. But send her nothing until I am gone. After all, men have been as bad as this and have recovered.' A beastly attitude, but that was Father.

"'I will tell you how Morstan died,' he continued. I am so sorry, Miss Morstan. Perhaps I ought to have softened the blow in some way, but I have always believed that quick and direct is the best way."

"It is all right," she said bravely. "I knew in my heart that he was dead."

"Father told us this: 'Morstan had suffered for years from a weak heart, but he concealed it from every one. I alone knew it. When in India, he and I, through a remarkable chain of circumstances, came into possession of a considerable treasure. I brought it over to England, and on the night of Morstan's arrival he came straight over here to claim his share. He walked over from the station and was admitted by my faithful old Lal Chowdar, who is now dead. Morstan and I had a difference of opinion as to the division of the treasure, and we came to heated words. Morstan had sprung out of his chair in a paroxysm of anger, when he suddenly pressed his hand to his side, his face turned a dusky hue, and he fell backward, cutting his head against the corner of the treasure-chest. When I stooped over him I found, to my horror, that he was dead.

"'For a long time I sat half distracted, wondering what I should do. My first impulse was, of course, to call for assistance; but I could not but recognize that there was every chance that I would be accused of his murder. His death at the moment of a quarrel, and the gash in his head, would be black against me. Again, an official inquiry could not be made without bringing out some facts about the treasure, which I was particularly anxious to keep secret. He had told me that no soul upon earth knew where he had gone. There seemed to be no necessity why any soul ever should know.

"'I was still pondering over the matter, when, looking up, I saw my servant, Lal Chowdar, in the doorway. He stole in and bolted the door behind him. "Do not fear, sahib," he said; "no one need know that you have killed him. Let us hide him away, and who is the wiser?" That was enough to decide me. If my own servant could not believe my innocence? Lal Chowdar and I disposed of the body that night, and within a few days the London papers were full of the mysterious disappearance of Captain Morstan. My fault lies in the fact that we concealed not only the body but also the treasure and that I have clung to Morstan's share as well as to my own. I wish you, therefore, to make restitution. Put your ears down to my mouth. The treasure is hidden in...'

"At this instant a horrible change came over his expression; his eyes stared wildly, his jaw dropped, and he yelled in a voice which I can never forget, 'Keep him out! For Christ's sake keep him out!' We both stared round at the window behind us upon which his gaze was fixed. A face was looking in at us out of the darkness. We could see the whitening of the nose where it was pressed against the glass. It was a bearded, hairy face, with wild cruel eyes and an expression of concentrated malevolence. My brother and I rushed towards the window, but the man was gone. When we returned to my father his head had dropped and his pulse had ceased to beat.

"We searched the garden that night but found no sign of the intruder save that just under the window a single footmark was visible in the flower-bed.

"The window of my father's room was found open in the morning, his cupboards and boxes had been rifled, and upon his chest was fixed a torn piece of paper with the words 'The sign of the four' scrawled across it."

"Did you by chance preserve this paper?" Holmes asked eagerly.

"Alas, I did not," Sholto admitted. "What the phrase meant or who our secret visitor may have been, we never knew. As far as we can judge, none of my father's property had been actually stolen, though everything had been turned out. My brother and I naturally associated this peculiar incident with the fear which haunted my father during his life, but it is still a complete mystery to us."

Sherlock Holmes leaned back in his chair with an abstracted expression and the lids drawn low over his glittering eyes.

"My brother and I," Sholto went on, "were, as you may imagine, much excited as to the treasure which my father had spoken of. For weeks and for months we dug and delved in every part of the garden without discovering its whereabouts. It was maddening to think that the hiding-place was on his very lips at the moment that he died. We could judge the splendor of the missing riches by the chaplet which he had taken out. I wanted to keep it with me, as I had taken a fancy to it, or so I told Bart. I foresaw great trouble between the two of us over this treasure, and I knew he would be averse to part with any of it, perhaps violently so. You see my brother is... Well, he is a troubled man, just as he was a troubled child. He has his own way of doing things, and it is not wise to cross him.

"Well, we finally located the hidden hoard. Our father had concealed it in the base of a stone fountain in the back garden. With that in hand, Bart forgot about the chaplet, which I kept in my own room. I took it upon myself to obtain Miss Morstan's address and send her a detached pearl at fixed intervals so that at least she might never feel destitute."

"It was a kindly thought," said Miss Morstan earnestly.

Sholto waved his hand deprecatingly.

A face was looking in at us out of the darkness.

"We were your trustees," he said. "That was the view which I took of it, though Bartholomew would never have seen it in that light. We had plenty of money ourselves, but there was never enough to suit *him*. I desired no more. Besides, it would have been such bad taste to have treated a young lady in so scurvy a fashion. '*Le mauvais goût mène au crime.*' The French have a very neat way of putting these things."

"*Bad taste leads to crime,*" Holmes translated.

"I would argue that bad taste *is* a crime," said Wilde, "and nine-tenths of the population dangerous criminals."

"Very droll, Mister Wilde," said Sholto. "Well, to make a long story at least a bit shorter, Bartholomew somehow learned that I had been sending pearls to Miss Morstan. Oh, what a row he raised over that! He has taken the chaplet from me and hidden the rest of the treasure away."

"Perhaps you could tell us a little more about your brother," Holmes said.

"It is an unfortunate story, Mister Holmes, one I wish could be wiped away. He has spent time in prison, sir. I am ashamed, but it is a matter of public record, and lying or withholding the information would be futile. It was a terrible scandal, and I credit it with our father's decline. He died shortly before Bart was released. My brother spent four years in *Wormwood* Scrubs while it was still under construction, as part of the convict labor gang. He was, by all accounts, a model prisoner. Would that he could have conducted himself in such an exemplary fashion both before and after his term of service, so that it would never have been necessary at all.

"It was a robbery in which Bart was involved in '77. Gold was stolen from an establishment called Hallward, I think it was. He was part of a small gang. Only two of the miscreants were apprehended, one of them being my poor brother. Bart was not the ringleader, and he claimed not to know the names of the men who were. Perhaps that was true, perhaps not. At any rate, he did not profit from it; none of them did. The proceeds were lost, and none of the conspirators, caught or uncaught, and whoever they might have been, realized a profit from the crime. It was justice of a sort, I suppose.

"I have tried to do what I could to steer Bart onto the right path, but he is incorrigible. He has been for as long as I can remember.

"I am his senior by almost seven minutes. He was actually stillborn. But, miraculously, he began to breathe. Our mother believed that another soul took possession of my brother's body during the time he lay as dead.

There was much talk of a man who had been hanged that very day. Mother believed that this man had taken refuge, as it were, in my brother's body."

Holmes came perilously close to rolling his eyes at this. I looked askance at it myself. Doyle, on the other hand, seemed intrigued.

"I know he has been involved in despicable things," Thaddeus Sholto went on. "Robberies, confidence tricks, even blackmail, a particularly loathsome crime, in my opinion."

"And you've no idea where he has hidden any of it?" said Holmes. "No clue at all?"

Sholto shrugged. "None, sir. He took the pearls from me, and now he has hidden the rest of the treasure somewhere. Possibly in this house, possibly elsewhere. He will not tell me. We must find it without his knowledge, do you see?"

"Yes," Holmes said thoughtfully. "Your brother, as you say, possesses a great deal of cunning. He knows that you want to locate the treasure. Tell me, knowing your brother as you do, where do you think the likeliest hiding-place is?"

"Well... He is quite territorial, and he regards the upper floors of this house as his domain. He has a great many safeguards in place to prevent me, or anyone else, from gaining access. That being the case, I am certain that he has the treasure up there somewhere. Frankly, I am afraid to go up there. I conduct all of my business down here. It is quite roomy enough. I have my little soirees, and Bart does not complain of the noise. He seems to take little notice of anything."

"Very well," Holmes said, nodding. "Then we may take it as a provisional hypothesis that the treasure is *not* hidden in Bartholomew Sholto's rooms."

"I would not have thought of that," said Thaddeus, "but it does make sense."

"I will be frank with you, Mister Sholto," said Holmes, "I offered to paint your portrait so that I could get inside this house without arousing suspicion. I have made my observations and it is plain to me that you have looked for the hiding-place here on the ground floor. Is this not so?"

"Well, yes, I have, but I didn't..."

"Never mind. It will not be in any obvious place. It may not be in the house at all."

"But Bartholomew never leaves the house."

"That you are aware of."

"Well, yes."

"Give me some time to consider," said Holmes. "Perhaps I can help you, Mister Sholto, along with Miss Morstan."

"I should be ever so grateful if you could, sir."

"What of the story he told us?" said Holmes, after we had left Pondicherry and were once again in the familiar milieu of Baker Street. We had stopped briefly at Mrs. Cecil Forrester's house to drop Miss Morstan off. Oscar Wilde had taken a cab back to his own home and family.

"It is rather difficult to take such a tale seriously," said Doyle. "But I don't think it should automatically be ruled out. I have heard far stranger things that turned out to be true.

"We certainly cannot dismiss it out of hand," Holmes said. "Whatever the facts are, it is possible that Thaddeus Sholto believes the tale he told us."

"He sounded sincere to me," I offered.

"That is unscientific, Watson," said Holmes. "And yet, I must confess that I received the same impression."

"One should not discount such feelings," said Doyle, "for they are based upon *something*. The mind collects a great deal of information every passing second, too much to sort through consciously and deliberately. I believe that such 'feelings' and 'impressions' may be based upon this in-formation, which is processed by the mind on a level that we do not fully understand."

"Well, then," said Holmes. "Let us say that Thaddeus Sholto is telling us the truth… or believes that he is. If he has been deceived, then the father was surely a party to it and on his deathbed no less."

"That is a bit difficult to navigate around," Doyle allowed.

"The father seems to have been a bit of a blackguard," said I.

"It is perhaps a pity that one cannot choose one's father," said Doyle. "I think I might have done a better job of it than nature did for me."

I agreed with him. To my surprise, Holmes gave a solemn nod, though he spoke not a word.

"One thing we certainly cannot get around," said I, "is the fact the pearls came from *somewhere*," I said.

"Oysters," Holmes muttered.

"Well, of course, but…"

"More information," Holmes said. "I must have more information.

Doctor Doyle, would you mind dispatching a telegram to Miss Morstan when you leave? Perhaps she knows more than she thinks she does."

Doyle agreed. After he had gone, Holmes sat for several minutes with his eyes closed and his fingertips pressed together.

"I have the very queer feeling, Watson," he said without opening his eyes, "that I know more than I think I know. How the devil do I throw a light upon it?"

CHAPTER ELEVEN
Holmes Receives an Envelope

iss Morstan arrived two hours later. Holmes questioned her at great length about her father and his friends and associations. This went on for more than two hours. If he gleaned anything valuable from it, he gave no indication.

Just as Holmes was preparing to end the interview, there came the sound of the bell, followed by the opening of the door downstairs. An excited babble of youthful voices arose, along with exclamations and admonitions from our long-suffering landlady. Several pairs of feet pounded up the seventeen steps and stopped outside our door.

Before a knock could sound, Holmes spoke, loudly enough to be heard in the hall:

"Come on in, lads, it isn't locked! And mind the noise!"

Into the room trooped three of the young Street Arabs Holmes had organized under the banner of the "Baker Street Irregulars."

"I have told you time and again," Holmes scolded, "to mind your manners when you come into this house. You can follow anybody through the streets of London without drawing attention to yourselves, why can you not enter these premises without giving poor Mrs. Hudson fits?"

"I tries to tell them this, Mister Holmes," said Wiggins, the oldest of the three, and the *de facto* leader of the Irregulars. "They're good lads, sir, but there is this unfortunate lack of discipline amongst them, which I believe to be a product of their upbringing. These old habits dies hard, you see, though I am ever vigilant over them and I entertains great hopes, sir."

Holmes, like myself, could not help but laugh. Miss Morstan stared at the boys as though they were creatures newly arrived from the moon.

"Very well," said Holmes, "But I expect to see some improvement one of these days. Now, what do you have for me?"

Wiggins stuck out his chest and proudly announced, "We have discovered the locality in which the man you told us to find resides in. It is a domicile, the address of which is writ down upon this here paper, sir."

"You did not approach him?"

"Certainly not, sir. You said not to, and we knows how to follow orders. When we are in our accustomed environment, that is to say, and doing the work for which we has trained so fervently."

"That is true. I apologize for casting aspersions, Wiggins."

"Oh, think nuffing of it sir. Whatever those are, you are forgiven for casting them. I am pleased to report that we caught sight of the subject in the King's Road not half an hour ago. He was walking unsteady-like, and my theory at present is that he was the worse for drink, in spite of the earliness of the hour. There are some men what cannot control their cravings, sir, as you know. We superstitiously trailed him to that address."

"I believe you mean *surreptitiously*, Wiggins."

"That may well be, sir."

"You have done very well, lads," said Holmes. "And what of the other matter? The house by the river."

"Yes, sir. I have had word from my lefftenant at the scene, and he reports no auspicious activity."

"Though you may be technically correct, Wiggins, I believe you mean *sus*picious."

"As you say, sir."

"Keep watch on Davies' place," said Holmes, "and get word to me immediately if he stirs."

"I doubts he'll be doing that any time soon, sir. He looked to have a right snootful. I knows whereof I speak on account of my old man, sir. Fathers can be difficult."

Holmes smiled sadly and touched the boy's head.

"Take care of yourself, Wiggins," he said softly.

"The Irregulars have located Pigeon Davies," he said to Miss Morstan, after the boys had been given two shillings each and had filled quietly out of the room and down to the street. "We shall just go have a little chat with him." He glanced at his watch. "There is no hurry. If he was, as the boys said, in his cups, I doubt he will stir from his bed any time soon.

"Perhaps we shall soon see some light at the end of the tunnel, Miss Morstan. My boys are also watching the little house on the Thames to which we traced the party who had been spying upon *this* house, and there has been no activity there so far. But the lads will stick with it, and when that party does return, we will know of it within minutes. But the man who tried to shoot you may give us all that we need."

"Yes, I do hope so," she said. "It is such a dark, dreadful business. I wish that I had never become involved."

"It was hardly your fault, Miss Morstan," said I. She made no response to this attempt of mine to bring her a bit of encouragement. Her pale face was like a porcelain mask. It was a somber young woman who said good-by to us; she seemed to have moved beyond hope into a shadow-land of perpetual fear and uncertainty.

"Perhaps we should notify the police, Holmes," I suggested after she had gone.

"I think not, Watson. For the moment, the police aren't to be trusted. Not on the whole, but one or two of them at present, and that is too many."

He had nothing further to say, and spent the next hour with his commonplace books, thumbing through them and muttering unintelligibly to himself. Whether he found any elucidation in them, I could not say. I busied myself with some personal correspondence. Presently there came a familiar tapping upon the door.

"This is for you, sir," said our landlady, when Holmes had answered her knock. "No return address, you see, nor a stamp, just your name written across the envelope. It had been pushed under the door, I don't know when."

"Well, what have we here?" Holmes said. He tore open the envelope and withdrew a folded sheet of paper. Spreading it open, he peered at it for a few seconds.

And then a very extraordinary thing happened.

Holmes' hand, the one in which he held the paper, shook. Only for a moment, but it was unmistakable. His eyes went wide, and what little color he had in his face drained away. He opened his mouth, then closed it. He was obviously in the grip of some strong emotion. I had never before observed such a thing! Throwing himself into his armchair, he closed his eyes and breathed deeply.

"What is it, Holmes?" I asked. "Bad news?"

"It is not news, Watson. Whether or not it is bad is a question I have struggled with for many a year. Does the word have any meaning in this context? I have managed to convince myself that it is neither bad nor good. It simply *is*."

After this, he fell silent, and I did not feel inclined to press him for an explanation of his extraordinary remarks. Though his agitation was palpable, I said nothing further to him.

I had never before seen Holmes in such a state. I managed to surreptitiously check the morocco case in which he kept his supply of cocaine and his needle, and saw that the level of fluid in the small bottle was the same as it had been two days previously. This relieved my mind on one score, but left me puzzled as to the source of his unusual agitation.

"I must see that man!" Holmes suddenly cried, jumping to his feet. "This is really too much. Come along, Watson, if you wish to. And bring your revolver!"

We walked through nameless streets, with grim, drab tenement buildings rearing up on both sides. I was quite lost, but Holmes, who seemingly carried a detailed street atlas in his brain, never faltered. Preoccupied though he appeared to be, his feet led us unerringly to our destination.

We stopped at a particular street corner and Holmes let out a low whistle. Within seconds, one of the Irregulars scampered out from behind a pile of dilapidated wooden crates stacked against a grimy brick wall and joined us.

"The man is in that building there," said the lad, pointing to a building halfway down the block. It was identical in every respect to its neighbors. "He's on the first floor. It's room number 12, but there's nothing on the door to show it. It's at the very end of the hallway, on the left."

"Excellent, Brownie," Holmes said, handing the boy a coin. "You've done well. I won't be needing you here any longer. Take this money and get yourself and your chums a good dinner somewhere. Meat and potatoes, mind you…not candy."

"Right ho, sir, thank you!" said the boy, giving a comical salute and disappearing into the mouth of a narrow alleyway.

"What now, Holmes?"

"Now," my friend said grimly, "I will get information from Davies, even if I must beat it out of him."

I was shocked. I had never heard Holmes express himself in such a way before. We went through the front door of the tenement. Seeing no one, we found the stairs and ascended.

It was the sort of dwelling that would have to undergo considerable improvements in order to be considered a hovel. It was not the worst the East End had to offer, but it was more than sufficient. I reached into my pocket and drew out my revolver.

We found room 12 at the end of the dark hallway. Holmes considered for a moment, then kicked the warped, flimsy door. The lock shattered, the metal doorknobs coming loose and bouncing across the floor.

A disheveled man sat up amidst a tangle of dirty sheets on a bed against the far wall. Before he could get his bearings, Holmes had him by the shirtfront.

"You will tell me what I wish to know, Davies."

I recognized the man as Miss Morstan's would-be assailant.

"Is that a fact, Mister Sherlock Holmes?" said the villain with a nasty leer. "You seem to know a great deal already. Do you really wish me to tell *everything* that I know? I possess some knowledge that you might not want your friend here to have."

Holmes narrowed his sharp gray eyes and said in a voice taut with anger, "To what do you refer, Davies?"

"I think you know, sir."

I thought I heard a noise from the hallway, but I could not be certain. I was cautiously backing around, never taking my eyes or my aim from Davies. I was sure now that I heard footsteps, and very unusual ones. There were two people approaching. Judging by the sound of their footfalls, a skill I acquired and honed in Afghanistan, one of them must have been shoeless, while the other... I was about to risk a glance at the doorway when matters took an unnerving turn.

Two dark figures rushed into the room. I turned my body and swung my pistol around to meet this new threat, if that's what it was, but I was too late. The figure in the lead, a man a bit taller than myself, caught me by the wrist with one hand and delivered a resounding blow to my cheek with the other.

I fell, twisting free from his grip and hanging on to my revolver, for all the good it did me.

A short but heavy wooden truncheon struck my wrist and the revolver was lost to me for the moment. The club had been wielded by the second figure to enter the room. This one was much shorter than the first, the size of a child, in fact. I did not pause to get a good look at this one, as the tall man seemed to be the greater threat. He had moved to confront Holmes.

Turning my attention in that direction, I saw that the man had a wooden leg. That explained the odd clomping sound I had heard coming up the hallway.

He was a sun-burned, reckless-eyed fellow, with a network of lines and wrinkles all over his mahogany features, which told of a hard, open-air life. There was a singular prominence about his bearded chin which marked a man who was not to be easily turned from his purpose.

He was grappling with Holmes, and I was prepared to spring forward and aid my friend, but something caught me from behind. I was pulled backward and lost my footing.

Holmes seemed to be getting the better of the first invader, but it was a near thing. Then the scale was tipped in the one-legged man's favor when the same individual who had waylaid me jumped onto Holmes' back and struck him several fierce blows on the head and neck.

Taking advantage of Holmes' moment of distraction, the one-legged man slammed him against the wall with terrific force, and turned to Davies.

"Thank God you've come," said the criminal. "I was afraid I might..."

That was all that Pigeon Davies had a chance to say. His final statement upon this earth would go unfinished. The wooden-legged man had produced a great, wicked knife from his belt and thrust it into Davies' chest. With a feeble cry, the killer-for-hire fell back onto the bed and lay still. The man who had just murdered him withdrew the knife from his heart.

Holmes, still stunned and unsteady, made a grab for him, but the fellow danced out of reach. His small companion caught him by the sleeve and began pulling him toward the door.

By this time, I was on my feet again, looking wildly about the room for my lost revolver. I did not see it, so I moved cautiously to Holmes' side, never taking my eyes from the queer invaders, whose backs were to me now. The tall man had reached the doorway, and the other turned to face us.

I could make neither heads nor tails of the creature that confronted us. It was about the size of an adolescent boy, very slim, with dark brown skin. Whether or not he was a genuine Negro I could not tell, as the palms of his hands and the soles of his feet were not visible. He wore short gloves and soft moccasins, and his head was covered by a strange hood with a tribal mask of some sort affixed to the front. This last appeared to be made of wood which had been carved into the semblance of a leering, demonic face, and painted in garish colors. The creature wore some kind of rough, sleeveless shirt and what appeared to be a grass skirt.

"What...what on earth are you?" I asked, somewhat stunned.

"I am TONGA," the creature announced in a weird, muffled voice. There was a small, oblong hole in the mask at the level of the mouth through which the queer words issued.

I looked at Holmes. He shook his head.

"I have no idea, Watson," he said, answering my unspoken question. To the apparition, he said:

"That is a most extraordinary costume you have constructed for yourself," he said calmly. "Though it is rather exotic-looking, I see no materials that could not be obtained very easily and cheaply here in London."

The creature made no reply, but the bearded man sprang forward, moving a bit awkwardly on his wooden leg. In his hand was the blood-streaked knife, which I now saw was of the type known as a *kukri*. In his other hand was a pistol. The only consolation I could find at that moment was the fact that the firearm was not mine...not that it was any less deadly.

"I've no quarrel with you two," said he in a low growl. "It means nothing to me whether you live or die. My little friend and I are going to leave here, and God willing we shall have no further dealings with you."

Holmes moved forward, and Tonga raised a strange device to the mouth aperture in his mask. I heard a puffing sound, and a small projectile issued from tube and struck Holmes upon the arm. He quickly took hold of it and plucked it out.

"It didn't break the skin," he said.

"Count yourself lucky," said the man. Brandishing his revolver at us, he made his exit, clomping off down the hallway with his queer companion at his heels.

"To follow them now would be suicide," Holmes said. "Are you all right, Watson?"

"Not really, Holmes, but I am alive and have suffered no permanent damage. What about you?"

"Well enough, though I believe my left canine tooth has been loosened. We shall have to summon the police, of course. But it would be as well that we not be found here, nor connected in any way with this murder. I shall just leave word with a certain party at Scotland Yard."

I scribbled a note to the police. Holmes gave it to one of the Irregulars, with instructions to deliver it to the nearest police-station without being seen. Then he suggested that I go back to Baker Street to rest and recuperate from my recent ordeal. For his part, he said rather ominously, he intended to have a talk with Mycroft.

"My brother seems to have shut himself off," Holmes said a few hours later, upon his return to our rooms. "I cannot gain an audience with him, which is more than curious. I believe he is avoiding me, Watson.

"The last I heard from him was that he had somehow quashed the inquiry into the Grand Duke's murder and that I need trouble myself with it no longer. Imagine that! What he is playing at, I cannot say."

"That is odd. But if he has managed to avoid an international incident, as he put it, then it must be for the best. Perhaps there are things he cannot tell you."

"That may be. He is better suited to that sort of intrigue than I am. I seek the truth; Mycroft must at times *conceal* the truth and seek the most plausible lie. The official story now is that his highness died of natural causes—a heart attack, I believe. It is fortunate for Mycroft's purposes that so few people know the true story."

"Just we two," said I. "and Athelney Jones. And Lestrade, of course."

Holmes nodded.

"Oh, by the way," he said absently, as though casually passing along a bit of trivia he had picked up somewhere, "I have learned one interesting fact that I neglected to mention; it might interest you to know that Thaddeus Sholto and his brother Bartholomew are identical twins."

Two more days passed, during which time Holmes pursued solitary researches and I attended to a few personal matters. On the evening of the second day, I made an inquiry of my friend:

"Still no word from your brother?"

"Nothing. But I have an interesting note from Lestrade. Before you ask, there is absolutely no doubt that he sent it. He and I have worked out a sort of cipher."

Chuck Miller

"When did you do that?"

"The night I was called away by the telegram purporting to be from him. A man named Ditter has been murdered. For more than twenty years, he operated a pawnbroking establishment. Utterly respectable on the surface, but it has long been suspected in certain quarters that he is a receiver of stolen goods. There is no great mystery about the killing, apart from the identity of the culprit. Ditter was shot dead, his cashbox emptied. Just another robbery turned tragic, Watson. It happens every day in this noble bastion of civilization, capital of the greatest empire ever wrought by the hand of man. Though Ditter dealt in all kinds of merchandise, he was believed to have specialized in precious stones—*and pearls*."

"It sounds simple enough," said I. "Why should Lestrade wish to consult you?"

"He does not. The case is not his, but he thought I would find it interesting. And I do, very much so. In fact, it is not his case. It was assigned originally to Lestrade, but another inspector requested it, and so it was reassigned."

"To whom?"

"Athelney Jones, Watson."

Later that evening, we received another disturbing bit of information, one that hit considerably closer to home. Miss Adler came to our rooms to inform us that Mary Morstan had not returned to the Forrester house upon the previous night, and now she was nowhere to be found.

We made efforts to locate her, but they bore no fruit. Miss Adler was beside herself. Holmes held a meeting with Inspector Lestrade; I was not invited to this colloquy, and do not know what, if anything, was decided upon. I knew that Holmes would not simply throw up his hands and accept our client's disappearance as a matter of course, but he did not make me privy to whatever course of action he decided upon.

CHAPTER TWELVE
The Testament of Jonathan Small

he following morning, another envelope arrived for Holmes. Again, Mrs. Hudson told us that it had been left upon the doorstep, in a similar manner to the letter that had caused my friend such agitation. He opened this new envelope, which was very large, and proved to contain a thick stack of note-paper held together by a metal clasp. He sat down to read.

Half an hour later Holmes passed the bundle of papers over to me.

"What on earth are we to make of this?" he sad.

I saw that the whole thing was printed in block letters, rather than cursive script. I took the bundle to my chair by the window, and read the following:

Dear Mister Sherlock Holmes:

They say you are more bulldog than man, and do not let go of a bone once you pick it up. Thus, I am making the choice to tell you all, and you may do what you wish with it. They also say you are fair, and I am counting on that. Once you have read my story, you will see that I am a wronged man and have only done what I've done to reclaim that which is mine. Judge me if you will, but I shan't submit to your judgment.

I am a Worcestershire man, born near Pershore. When I was about eighteen, I took the Queen's shilling and joining the Third Buffs, which was just starting for India.

I had got past the goose-step and learned to handle my musket, when I got involved in a bit of foolishness that almost cost me everything. One night I had been out drinking and I did quite a thorough job of it. I fell in with a pair of officers whose names I did not get. We were all joviality and good spirits, or so I thought. They treated me as their equal, and that just went to my head, if the truth be told.

Our little spree went on for some time, until I found myself, all of a sudden as it seemed, prowling on the banks of the Ganges with my countrymen. It was then that they clouted me over the head and stole all of the money I had. This was not quite enough for them, however, and to top the evening off, they pitched me into the river. I came to and started to swim for the other side. A crocodile took me just as I was halfway across and nipped off my right leg just above the knee. I got away with my life, but I was five months in hospital over it, and when at last I was able to limp out with this timber toe strapped to my stump, I found myself invalided out of the Army and unfitted for any active occupation.

But a man named Abel White, who had come out there as an indigo-planter, wanted an overseer to look after his coolies. He happened to be a friend of our colonel's, who recommended me for the post.

It was not long after I began that the great mutiny broke upon us. Our plantation was at a place called Muttra. Day after day we had small companies of Europeans passing through our estate on their way to Agra, where were the nearest troops. Abel White was an obstinate man, and he decided to stay planted. Well, one fine day the crash came. I had been away, and was riding home in the evening, when I saw thick smoke curling up from Abel White's bungalow and the flames beginning to burst through the roof. From where I stood I could see hundreds of the black fiends, dancing and howling round the burning house.

I broke away across the paddy-fields, and found myself late at night safe within the walls at Agra.

Alas, there was no safety there, either. The whole country was up like a swarm of bees. At Agra there were the Third Bengal Fusiliers, some Sikhs, two troops of horse, and a battery of artillery. A volunteer corps of clerks and merchants had been formed, and this I joined, wooden leg and all. We went out to meet the rebels at Shahgunge, and beat them back for a time, but our powder gave out, and we had to fall back upon the city.

We were lost among the narrow, winding streets. Our leader moved across the river, therefore, and took up his position in the old fort of Agra. It is enormous. There is a modern part, which took our entire garrison, women, children, stores, and everything else. But the modern part is nothing like the size of the old quarter, where nobody goes, and which is full of great deserted halls and winding passages. It is a haunted place, I think, with ancient intrigues lurking in every dark corner, the living and the dead all together, and never knowing which is which.

There are many doors, and these had to be guarded. We were short-handed, and it was impossible for us to station a strong guard at every one of the innumerable gates. We organized a central guardhouse in the middle of the fort, and arranged to leave each gate under the charge of one white man and two or three natives. I was selected to take charge of an isolated door upon the south-west side of the building. Two Sikh troopers were placed under my command.

For two nights I kept the watch with two brothers called Mahomet and Abdullah, both old fighting men. They were a strange pair, difficult to read, with something sinister shared between the two of them. If one was good and the other bad, I could not tell which was which. They could talk English pretty well, but were not inclined to do it much with me.

The third night of my watch was dark and dirty, with a small driving rain. There might have been a few centuries' worth of ghosts drifting about out there in the downpour. Finding that my companions would not be led into conversation, I took out my pipe and laid down my musket to strike the match. In an instant the two Sikhs were upon me. Abdullah snatched my firelock up and leveled it at my head, while Mahomet held a knife to my throat.

"Don't make a noise," he hissed.

"Listen to me, sahib," said Abdullah. "You must be with us now, or be silenced forever. I would as soon kill you, but my brother is a compassionate man, and he has persuaded me. The thing is too great a one for us to hesitate. Either you are with us on your oath on the cross of the Christians, or your body this night shall be thrown into the ditch. There is no middle way. Which is it to be?"

"You have not told me what you want of me," said I. "If it is anything against the safety of the fort…"

"It is nothing against the fort," said he. "We only ask you to do that which your countrymen come to this land for…to be rich. If you will be one of us, we will swear to you that you shall have your fair share of the loot. A quarter of it shall be yours."

"But what is the treasure ?" I asked.

"Will you swear," said he, "to raise no hand and speak no word against us?"

"I will," I answered.

"Then you shall have a quarter of the treasure which shall be equally divided among the four of us."

"There are but three," said I.

"Dost Akbar must have his share. We can tell the tale to you while we wait for him.

"There is a rajah in the northern provinces who has much wealth, though his lands are small. He is of a low nature and hoards his gold. And, in truth, he had earned none of it. He was a thief, plain and simple, that's how he got his start as a man of means. Years before the current troubles, he stole a load of valuables that were being moved under guard from one outpost to another. I don't know any more details about that, who he stole from, or what, if anything, they tried to do about it. Then, clever devil that he was, he went up and down the country trading his loot for other valuable objects, banknotes, what have you, so that if he were caught there would be nothing to connect him to the original theft. He carried on in this fashion for some time, trading back and forth and across the borders, until he had quite a hoard, all of it in stones and precious metals.

"When the troubles broke out he would be friends with both the sepoy *and* with the Company's raj. He made such plans that come what might; half at least of his treasure should be left to him. That which was in gold and silver he kept in his palace, but the most precious stones that he had he put in an iron box and sent it by a servant, who, under the guise of a merchant, should take it to the fort at Agra. If the rebels won he would have his money, but if the Company conquered, his jewels would be saved.

"This pretended merchant, who travels under the name of Achmet, is now in the city of Agra and desires to gain his way into the fort. He has with him our foster-brother Dost Akbar, who knows his secret. Dost Akbar has promised to lead him this very night to a side-postern of the fort, and has chosen this one for his purpose. Here he will find us waiting. The world shall know the merchant Achmet no more, and the treasure of the rajah shall be divided among us. What say you?"

"I am with you," said I.

"It is well," he answered. "We have now only to wait. We will to the gate now and keep watch."

The rain was still falling steadily, and it was hard to see more than a stonecast. Suddenly I saw the glint of a shaded lantern at the other side of the deep moat that lay in front of our door; the water was in places nearly dried up, and it could easily be crossed.

"Here they are!" I exclaimed.

"Challenge him as usual," whispered Abdullah. "Send us in with him, and we shall do the rest."

The light flickered onward until I could see two dark figures upon the other side of the moat. I let them scramble down the sloping bank and climb halfway up to the gate before I challenged them. They looked like a pair of drowned sailors rising from the deep.

"Who goes there?" said I.

"Friends," came the answer. I uncovered my lantern and threw a flood of light upon them. The first was an enormous Sikh, and the other was a

"Who goes there?"

little fat fellow with a great yellow turban and a bundle in his hand.

"Your protection, sahib," he panted, "for the unhappy merchant Achmet. I have been robbed and beaten because I am a friend of the Company."

"What have you there?" I asked.

"An iron box," he answered, "which contains one or two little family matters which I should be sorry to lose."

"Take him to the main guard," said I. The two Sikhs closed in upon him on each side, and the giant walked behind, while they marched in through the gateway.

I could hear their footsteps sounding through the lonely corridors. Suddenly it ceased, and I heard voices and a scuffle, with the sound of blows. A moment later there came a rush of footsteps coming in my direction. I turned my lantern down the long straight passage, and there was the fat man, running like the wind and close at his heels was the great black-bearded Sikh, with a knife in his hand. The fat man was gaining ground, so I cast my firelock between his legs as he raced past, and he rolled twice over like a shot rabbit. Then the Sikh was upon him and took the poor bastard's head almost clean off with his great, broad knife.

We carried him in, to a place which the Sikhs had prepared, in a winding passage that led to a great empty hall. The earth floor had sunk in at one place, so we left Achmet there, covered with loose bricks.

We opened the box, and the light of the lantern gleamed upon a collection of gems such as I had never imagined. There were diamonds and emeralds; rubies and carbuncles; and nearly three hundred very fine pearls.

We agreed to conceal our loot in a safe place until the country should be at peace again. There was no use dividing it at present, for if gems of such value were found upon us it would cause suspicion. We carried the box into the hall where we had buried the body, and hid it away.

After Wilson took Delhi and Sir Colin relieved Lucknow the back of the business was broken. Fresh troops arrived. A flying column reached to Agra and cleared the Pandies away. Peace seemed to be settling upon the country, and we four were beginning to hope that our time was at hand.

In a moment, however, our hopes were shattered by our being arrested as the murderers of Achmet.

When the rajah put his jewels into the hands of Achmet he did it because he knew that he was a trusty man. Then he took a second even more trusty servant and set him to spy upon the first. He went after Achmet that night and saw him pass through the doorway. Of course he thought he had taken refuge in the fort and applied for admission there himself next day, but could find no trace of Achmet. He spoke to a sergeant of guides, who spoke to the commandant. A search was made, and the body discovered. We were all four seized and brought to trial on a charge of murder; three of us because we had held the gate that night, and the fourth because he was known to have been in the company of the murdered man. Not a word about the jewels came out. The Sikhs got penal servitude for life, and I was condemned to death, though my sentence was afterwards commuted to the same as the others.

There we were, tied by the leg with no chance of getting out. I just held on and bided my time.

At last it seemed to come. I was changed from Agra to Madras, and from there to Blair Island in the Andamans. There are very few white convicts at this settlement, and I soon found myself a sort of privileged person. I learned to dispense drugs for the surgeon, and picked up a smattering of his knowledge. All the time I was on the lookout for a chance to escape.

The surgeon, Dr. Somerton, and the other young officers would meet in his rooms of an evening and play cards. Among the regulars were a Major Sholto and a Captain Morstan, who were in command of the native troops; a youngish fellow the others referred to as the Grand Duke; the surgeon himself; and two or three prison-officials, crafty old hands who played a nice sly game.

In these games, the soldiers used always to lose and the civilians to win. These prison-chaps had done little else than play cards ever since they had been there. Night after night the soldiers got up poorer men, and the poorer they got the more keen they were to play. Major Sholto was the hardest hit.

One night he lost more heavily than usual. I was sitting in my hut when he and Morstan came stumbling by. They were bosom friends, those two. The major was raving about his losses.

"It's all up, Morstan," he was saying. "I am a ruined man."

"Nonsense!" said the other. "I've had a nasty facer myself, but..." That was all I could hear, but it set me thinking.

A couple of days later, I took the chance of speaking to him.

"I wish to have your advice, Major," said I. "Who is the proper person to whom hidden treasure should be handed over? I know where half a million worth lies, and, I thought perhaps the best thing would be to hand it over to the proper authorities."

"Half a million?" he gasped.

"Quite that, sir, in jewels and pearls. The real owner is outlawed and cannot hold property, so it belongs to the first comer. Should I give the information to the governor-general?"

"Well, you had best let me hear all about it," said he.

I told him my story, keeping back some of the details.

"This is a very important matter," he said when I had finished. "You must not say a word to anyone." At that moment, I knew I had him.

Two nights later he and Captain Morstan came to my hut in the dead of the night. "We have been talking it over," said the major, "and my friend and I have come to the conclusion that this secret of yours is not a government matter, but a private concern of your own. We wish to help you, but we will, of course, expect some kind of compensation. What price would you ask?"

"There is only one bargain which a man in my position can make. I shall want you to help me to my freedom, and my three companions to theirs."

"How can we?"

"I have thought it all out. The only bar to our escape is that we can get no fit boat. There are plenty of little yachts and yawls at Calcutta or Madras which would serve. Bring one over; we shall get aboard her by night, and if you will drop us on any part of the Indian coast you will have done your part of the bargain, and my friends and I will cut you in."

"It's a dirty business," Morstan said to Sholto. "But the money will save our commissions."

"Well," said the major, "we must try and meet you. Tell me where the box is hid, and I shall get leave of absence and go back to India to make inquiries."

"Not so fast," said I. "I must have the consent of my three comrades."

The matter was ended by a second meeting, at which Mahomet, Abdullah, and Dost Akbar were present. We were to provide charts of the part of the Agra fort, and mark the place where the treasure was hid. Major Sholto was to go to India to test our story. If he found the box he was to leave it there, to send out a small yacht provisioned for a voyage, which was to lie off Rutland Island, and to which we were to make our way, then return to his duties. Captain Morstan would apply for leave of absence, to meet us at Agra, where we would have a final division of the treasure, he taking the major's share and his own.

Sholto went to India, but he never came back. Captain Morstan said that Sholto's uncle had died, leaving him a fortune, and he had left the Army. That was the story Sholto told, at any rate. And when Sholto left, he was accompanied by this Grand Duke. That was the only name I had for that particular gentleman at the time, but I have since learned his true identity and station.

Morstan went over to Agra shortly afterwards and found that the treasure was indeed gone. The scoundrel had stolen it all! He had no qualms about deceiving his brother officer and making off with the treasure that he should have shared. Morstan was thunderstruck. Funny how you can have a man by your side most of your life, and look upon him as a brother, only to learn that he is the opposite of what he presents himself to be! From that I lived only for vengeance. After all that I had endured, the treasure might as well have gone into the river with my missing leg.

But it was weary years before my time came. One day when Dr. Somerton was down with a fever a little Andaman Islander was picked up by a convict-gang in the woods. He was sick to death and had gone to a lonely place to die. I took him in hand, and after a couple of months I got him all right and able to walk. He took a kind of fancy to me then. I had seen him initially as a fierce, deadly little chap, but I soon learned that first impressions are not to be trusted. Though he was generally sullen and serious, there was something childlike, even merry about him, if you knew how to look for it.

Tonga, for that was his name, was a fine boatman and owned a big, roomy canoe of his own. When I found that he would do anything to serve me, I saw my chance of escape. I talked it over with him. He was to bring his boat round on a certain night to an old wharf which was never guarded, to pick me up.

At the night named he had his boat at the wharf, and soon we were well out at sea. On the eleventh day we were picked up by a trader which was going from Singapore to Jiddah with a cargo of Malay pilgrims. They were a rum crowd, but they let you alone and asked no questions.

Here and there we drifted about the world, and at last we found ourselves in England. I had no great difficulty in finding where Sholto lived, and I soon found that he still had the jewels. Then I tried to get at him in many ways; but he was pretty sly and had always two prize-fighters, besides his sons and his khitmutgar, on guard over him. Morstan was dead, I learned, and I had no way of tracing the mysterious Grand Duke. For all I knew, both of them had been murdered by the treacherous dog who I had come to have it out with.

One day, I got word that Sholto was dying. I hurried at once to the garden, mad that he should slip out of my clutches like that, and, looking through the window, I saw him lying in his bed, with his sons on each side of him. Even as I looked at him his jaw dropped, and I knew that he was gone. I got into his room that same night, though, and I searched his papers to see if there was any record of where he had hidden our jewels. There was not a line. I came away, bitter and savage as a man could be. Before I left I bethought me that if I ever met my Sikh friends again it would be a satisfaction to know that I had left some mark of our hatred; so I scrawled down the sign of the four of us, and I pinned it on his bosom.

But I knew those two boys of his could put their hands on the loot very quickly, if they had the right persuasion applied to them. What I learned about the pair was that they were as different as night and day. Thaddeus was essentially a good lad, if a bit foolish. His brother, Bartholomew, was something else again. A regular villain he was, having done time in prison for his part in a robbery, and no telling what all he did that he never got caught for. I spent time studying them and learned a lot of interesting things, but not the location of the treasure.

At some point, however, they found it, which I learned of in a way that I prefer not to reveal to you. I was encouraged by this, but before I could act, there were developments.

Poor Thad had kept back some pearls, which he had been sending to Miss Morstan. When Bart learned of it, he flew into a rage and made threats and hid the treasure away. I was trying to work out a course of action when you became involved all of a sudden. I scarcely knew what to think. I know something of you, and was afraid that you would locate the treasure before I could, and all would be lost. What was I to do?

The Grand Duke was in it, too, and we scared him off. You might question him, but he'd never admit to anything.

To top all of this off, Bartholomew learned about me and decided that the world would be a better place without me in it. He sent a hired man, the same one he had employed in his attempt to eliminate Miss Morstan, after Tonga and me. His attempt to do away with us failed, and we finally managed to track him to his lair. You know how that played out, Mister Holmes. He brought his demise on himself. The same goes for a chap named Ditter, who had some mysterious connection to the Sholtos. I never found out exactly what that was, though I have ideas. The scoundrels depended on Ditter in some of their other dirty work, so I removed him, and I am not sorry I did it.

If there were some clever way to save the situation, I would take it. But it is time at last to admit that the treasure is lost to me forever. History will repeat itself, and am I then to cast my pearls into the dark, deep waters? Best Tonga and I go back where we came from, and have no further truck with the Sholto household or Mister Sherlock Holmes. I can further assure you, to ease your mind if that is necessary, that Miss Morstan is unharmed. I persuaded her to leave town for just a few days, while this business played out. Now it is done as far as I am concerned, and she will turn up in due course. I hope never to see or hear of any of you lot again, the devil may have you, for my part.

--Jonathan Small
Late of Her Majesty's Army and Other Indignities

"Dash it all," said Holmes, "this complicates matters. Printing is a great deal more difficult to analyze than cursive script. Indeed, I have never had occasion to attempt it. I can make only a few deductions.

"The majority of these papers have been torn from a note-book, and are of a uniform age. You can see that they are quite yellowed. But look at the ink. On the first three pages of the main narrative, it is faded. It has been on this paper for many years. Ten or twelve at least, if I'm any judge. But notice the rest. The printing is the same; there are two or three minor discrepancies, but it was surely done by the same hand; and the ink is certainly a close match, but it is much newer. This also holds true for the cover letter. These pages have been inscribed within the last month at most, Watson, probably the last few days."

"Well," said I, "it seems plain that this fellow wrote up his account very recently, as he says in the letter. He probably used whatever paper came to hand."

"That sounds plausible, but it will not do. As you know, I have made exhaustive studies of various types of paper and ink. There are three or four of my little monographs on the shelf by the basket-chair. Look here: The final page is on different paper altogether! Very similar, but subtly different. The ink is the same, as is the printing, so far as I can be certain. And not only the last page, but a few of the interior pages are on this mismatched paper as well. What have they in common?"

He went back through the strange narrative page by page, uttering little exclamations here and there. "Oh, yes, I do see... clever... Oh, very neat! Yes, I believe I understand now. You knew that I would, I'll wager!"

"To whom are you speaking, Holmes?"

"To the writer of this grotesque account, Watson. I believe I understand the situation now…to a degree."

"It seems straightforward enough."

"That is exactly what it is *not*. I am dealing with a very nimble mind, Watson, and I must be careful how I take my cues. It is complicated, and I do not wish to make any pronouncements until I am sure. Which will be soon. If my suppositions are correct, the end must come soon."

"I do not understand."

"Perhaps events will remedy that condition before too much more time has passed. Would you please step down to the street and give a brief whistle? One of the Irregulars is stationed nearby and he will hear you and show himself. I just need to write a brief note and give it to him to deliver."

After this little operation had been completed, I asked a question that had begun to nag at me:

"If the Grand Duke was involved in this treasure scheme, what are we to make of the blackmail attempt and murder?"

"The latter fits the scenario quite well but the former does not. Not if one applies *ordinary* logic. But, as I am beginning to learn, there are other kinds."

Holmes fell into a brown study. I glanced over at the mantelpiece and saw that the morocco case appeared to be undisturbed. That was good. Holmes, in spite of his obvious agitation, had not turned to his drugs for comfort.

I thought I knew why Holmes had not taken me into his confidence about the letter he had received. It seemed plain to me that he was now being blackmailed by our adversary. I knew that such a pointed reminder of his own personal vulnerability would not sit well with him.

I suggested that we go out for something to eat, but Holmes would not hear of it.

"No, Watson, here we must remain. We cannot be out of pocket when the final hand is played. There is much at stake here."

"Do you think Small is telling the truth about Miss Morstan?"

"That is an intriguing question. If this document is what I think it is, then Miss Morstan is alive. Whether or not she is safe remains to be seen."

I did not bother to ask Holmes for an explanation, for I knew from long experience how far that would get me. I merely took what little comfort I could in his cryptic words.

With Sherlock Holmes, that was often the best one could hope for. All would be made clear, but Holmes would set the schedule for it, not I.

CHAPTER THIRTEEN
The River Chase

he wooden-legged man and the savage have turned up at the waterfront building," said young Wiggins, "and they have been there for no more than half an hour."

The boy had arrived at our door, excited and out of breath, with his news.

Holmes and I donned our jackets and followed the boy downstairs. We leapt into a hansom cab and were off, quick as a flash, to the little brick house on the Thames. Wiggins seemed to enjoy the cab ride immensely; it was plain that he had never possessed the wherewithal for such extravagances.

We disembarked from the cab in front of the Smith house. Young Jack, standing in the doorway, waved to us, and we joined him.

"Smitty here has something to tell you," said Wiggins. Turning to the boy, he said, "Remember, Smitty, if you want to serve with the Irregulars, you must speak respectfully to our chief, Mister Holmes, and his friends. No foolishness, and no asking for money. You'll be paid as you do your job."

"That man come back again the other day," the boy said. "The one my mum told you about. I seen him too, more than once. But this last time... Well, he was *different*. It was the look on his face, Mister Holmes. It was like as if the devil had come out of him. He still had the same kind of looks about him, you know, like my mum told you before, but his eyes was different. He was just an ordinary man, sir, without all that evil about him."

"That is very interesting. Had he anything with him when he went into the building?"

"Quite right he did. A box. More of a chest I suppose, but not one of them large ones."

"Was he alone?"

"I think so, sir."

"Very well. Jack, go tell your father to make ready. I believe we may have need of the *Aurora* very soon."

"I believe all is in readiness," said Holmes. "It is time to play out the last act of this little drama. I am eager to see the result. There is the house. They have been in there for some little time. There is unlikely to be any genuine danger, but we must act as though there were."

We burst through the door, into the dank interior of the house, which would be better described as a noisome shack. Standing close to the rear wall were Jonathan Small and the grotesque little Tonga.

"Blast it, here they are," said the former. "To the boat, Tonga! We shall get away with it yet!"

Small had a pistol in one hand and with the other, he clutched a wooden cask to his chest. It was about two feet long, a foot wide, and six or eight inches deep.

"So," Holmes said mockingly, "you have put your hands on the treasure after all, eh, Small?"

Small had his pistol, as did Holmes and I. Tonga held his lethal blowpipe. It was a standoff, and neither faction had an appreciable advantage.

Our adversaries stepped cautiously to the door through which Holmes and I had just entered, keeping us covered with their weapons. It was plain that we must let them go, or risk a skirmish that could be fatal to all present.

Once outside, the pair moved rapidly to the wharf, and climbed down into a trim little launch that was moored there.

"They'll be off, then," said Holmes. "This must play out as my correspondent has planned it. Have faith that we are not misled. Let's get to Smith's place. He should be ready for us."

We walked briskly to the Smith house. Young Jack was standing out front, waving to us.

"Come, gentlemen!" he shouted. "Father has the *Aurora* ready!"

We followed the boy out onto the wharf and climbed down into the *Aurora*. Holmes and I shook hands with Smith.

"She's ready to go, Mister Holmes," said he. "The other boat has a bit of a start on us, but my girl here can keep up with her, no fear."

We set out, the boy Jack on the tiller, Smith shoveling coal into the boiler.

"That launch is swifter than she looks," said Smith. "I've never seen her before. Wonder where she's from?"

The boat was larger and flatter than the *Aurora*, and was painted a flat, somber black. As we moved out into the river, I could see that she was churning up a nice little wake.

"Our opponent has resources," said Holmes. "But he also has serious liabilities, of which I doubt he is fully aware."

Smith shoveled more coal into the boiler and we fell in behind the other craft. Holmes seemed oddly relaxed. He sat upon the low bench that ran along one side of the deck, head thrown back, eyes half-closed, for all the world as though he were enjoying a holiday at Brighton.

Before long, we were fairly after the other boat. The *Aurora's* engines whizzed and clanked like a great metallic heart. Her sharp, steep prow cut through the still river-water and sent two rolling waves to right and to left of us. With every throb of the engines we sprang and quivered like a living thing. One great yellow lantern in our bows threw a long, flickering funnel of light in front of us.

Right ahead a dark blur upon the water showed where Small's boat lay, and the swirl of white foam behind her spoke of the pace at which she was going.

"Don't overdo it, Smith!" said Holmes. "We just need to keep them within sight, that's all."

"Right, sir."

"I think we gain a little," said young Jack from his place at the tiller.

"I am sure of it," said I. "We shall be up with her in no time."

At that moment, as fate would have it, a tug with three barges in tow blundered in between us. It was only by putting our helm hard down that we avoided a collision, and before we could round them and recover our way the other boat had gained a good two hundred yards. She was still, however, well in view, and the murky, uncertain twilight was settling into a clear, starlit night. The low clouds that had hung over the city for so many days had departed, their promise of rain unfulfilled.

Suddenly, Small's boat swung around and headed back toward us. Smith yelled for the boy to get us out of the other craft's path, and he barely managed to do so. Once we were safe, the boy turned the *Aurora* around, and we were heading back the way we had come.

When our course had been corrected, young Jack held the tiller steady, while his father, stripped to the waist, shoveled coals into the boiler.

We drew so close that we could plainly see the figures upon her deck. Jonathan Small stood near the prow, while the abominable Tonga operated the tiller.

Holmes had already drawn his revolver, and I whipped out mine at the sight of the weird, distorted creature.

"Don't fire on the savage," said Holmes quietly, "whatever you do."

We were within a boat's-length by this time, and almost within touch of our quarry. Then it was half a boat's length, then just a couple of feet.

It was then that I did something very reckless, not to say foolish,with no clear idea of why I was doing it. What mad impulse impelled me, I cannot say even now, but as the two boats drew closer together, I balanced myself on the prow of the *Aurora* and leapt through the air onto the deck of the other craft. Holmes shouted in alarm, but I was already away.

Astonishingly, I found and kept my footing on the other deck, and found myself face-to-face with Jonathan Small.

"Where is Miss Morstan?" I demanded. "What have you done with her? If she has been harmed..."

I raised my pistol, but the deck shifted beneath my feet at that moment and spoiled my aim. In an instant, Small was upon me

"You are an irritant, Doctor," he said through clenched teeth. "But you will not be difficult to remove."

By this time, Small's boat had surged forward and cut abruptly to the left, putting several yards between us and the *Aurora*.

Small forced me down onto the deck, his full weight upon my chest and stomach. I lost my revolver then. Small reached into his belt and produced a large, flat-bladed knife. I caught hold of his wrist, but his arm was stronger than mine. I could not prevent him from cutting my throat.

At that moment, a strange sort of peace enveloped my soul. Death had come, I believed, and there was no sense railing against it. In the next few seconds I would cease to be, or else I would go to join my departed family. Neither prospect was attractive. But, as I had learned in Afghanistan, one must always be ready to accept the inevitable. As Jonathan Small's knife touched my throat, I closed my eyes and let my mind go blank.

But this was not to be the day that I kept my appointment with Eternity. Salvation came to me in a most unexpected form.

I heard Small cry out and I opened my eyes. My attacker had scrambled to his feet and stood above me, knife hand dangling at his side. With his other hand, he was plucking a small thorn from his neck.

"You fool!" he roared, whirling to face Tonga. "Do you want to kill me?" He flung the thorn toward the water. "I don't think there was time for me to absorb much of the poison, thank God!"

I could not be certain, but I thought I heard a familiar female utter a single, horrified word: "What?" By this time, I had gotten up from the deck, ignoring the pain in my game leg. I struck Small in the face with my fist.

Small shook off my blow and advanced upon me with the knife held out. I backed toward the railing. It seemed that my appointment had merely been postponed for a moment. The launch, out of control now, encountered some sort of turbulence and began lurching this way and that.

Tonga picked up the wooden cask we had observed earlier and flung it at Small; it struck the peg-legged scoundrel in the head, knocking him off balance and over the rail. He managed to hang on with his free hand. The cask hit the water with a splash and vanished. Whatever it contained was obviously heavy enough to pull it under.

Instinctively, I moved to assist Small. Villain or no, I had taken a vow to preserve life wherever possible. In the excitement, I overlooked that fact that Small had most certainly never taken such an oath. He transferred his grip from the railing to my arm and swung again with his knife. The blade slashed through my jacket and I felt a stinging sensation across my shoulder.

I pulled myself backward, drawing Small back over the railing, and fell to the deck once more. Small lost his balance momentarily, but soon righted himself and stood over me, preparing for a downward plunge with the knife.

And then something extraordinary happened.

Tonga barreled across the deck and struck Small, knocking him backward and away from me. But this was not enough for the little savage, who struggled fiercely to push Small back to the railing and over it. My adversary was taken quite by surprise, and the whole business was over before I could react.

Small and Tonga tumbled over the rail together and plunged into the dark water.

What happened after that is a confused jumble in my mind. I can recall being surprised to find myself sitting upon the deck rather than standing, with no memory of the transition. Vaguely conscious of a stinging pain, I touched my shoulder; my hand came away wet, and not with river water. Holmes had managed to jump onto Small's boat, and had gotten it under control. Then I was on my feet, and Holmes was examining my wound. "It is not bad, old man, thank God. We must clean and bandage it."

And then we were back aboard the *Aurora*. Smith had turned the launch around and headed back toward his home. I can recall how the cool air felt blowing across my face, the smell of it, how it soothed me… but nothing else.

Next, I was conscious of Mrs. Smith putting a blanket around my shoulders and leading me to a bench near the water. She relieved me of my torn and blood-stained shirt, giving me a rough work-shirt that belonged to her husband.

My unbroken memories resume upon that bench, as I squirmed inside the ill-fitting, but blessedly dry, shirt.

"The treasure has gone into the Thames," said Holmes as he sat down next to me. "So have Jonathan Small and his malevolent imp. In the unlikely event that either of them have survived, they should not be difficult to spot. It is more likely, however, that the bodies will wash ashore eventually."

Holmes told me he had sent word to Athelney Jones. That puzzled me. I knew that he disliked Jones and distrusted him. I was astonished that he did not summon Lestrade, with whom he seemed to have formed a particular bond in recent days. It also occurred to me that Holmes had made no effort to summon Jones or anyone else before we stormed the little brick house.

Be that as it may, the case of Jonathan Small and the fiendish Tonga came to a close. We handed the Testament over to Jones, who seemed delighted to receive it. The murders of the Grand Duke and the underworld merchant Ditter could be closed. The river would be dragged for the two bodies, but no one seemed in a hurry to commence that operation.

"It seems that all of our little mysteries are solved," said Holmes. "But, like Prince Hamlet, I place little stock in that which *seems*. I believe we have discussed this before, Watson. I am not satisfied, not satisfied at all. Not yet, at any rate."

"Athelney Jones seems to be satisfied."

"I fancied that he would. It would be a satisfactory outcome from his point of view, to be sure. Everything tied up neatly. And, for the second time in his career, most of the evidence in a criminal case has ended up at the bottom of the Thames, never to be seen again. It is becoming quite a habit with him."

"Well, you have brought about a conclusion, whether or not it is universally satisfying."

"I do hope I have done the right thing, Watson. I had to try to salvage something for the poor creature that wrote that 'testament,' if only the illusion of self-respect."

"I do not understand," said I, "and I believe you know that. When are you going to make this clear to me?"

"In time, Watson. It is said that everything will be made clear in time. The Scriptures promise that, do they not?"

CHAPTER FOURTEEN
Poor Little Tonga

We spent a pleasant interval in the Smith home, recovering from our exertions. The house was small, but cozy and inviting. My wound was not serious at all. Mrs. Smith insisted on feeding us some stewed pork and black bread, to which I did justice. Holmes, whose eating habits are generally unpredictable, did the same.

After he finished eating, Holmes whispered a few instructions to young Jack, who hastened from the house to carry them out. Within a very few minutes, the boy returned, and stood in the doorway beckoning Holmes to get up.

"Watson," said my friend, "if you're feeling up to it, let's take a little stroll."

I rose and followed him out, past the end of the wharf, and down onto the embankment. Young Jack strode along, a few yards ahead of us.

"There they are," said he, pointing to a cluster of figures perhaps a tenth of a mile distant. He scampered off in their direction, leaving Holmes and myself to keep up as best we could.

We approached a small knot of boys, whom I recognized as three of the Baker Street Irregulars. The leader of the band, young Wiggins, was holding an odd-looking wooden object perhaps a foot and a half in length and fitted out with several leather straps.

"I don't know what it is," said one of the boys. "Perhaps it's a cricket bat of some sort. Why does it have these straps on it?"

"Wiggins!" Holmes called out. "What have you there?"

The boy looked around and waved. "That's what I'm trying to figger out just at present, Mister Holmes, sir. We have discovered this queer-looking object and have been debating about its identity and purpose."

"Hand it here, and let me see if I cannot enlighten you."

Holmes examined the thing with his magnifying-glass. The Irregulars stood around him, looking on in awe, as though my friend were an alchemist who was about to change the wood into gold.

"Do you think it belonged to Jonathan Small, Holmes?" I asked, regretting it almost instantly. I nodded to acknowledge that I deserved the look of mild scorn Holmes gave me. There was no doubt that this object was Small's wooden leg. It had somehow come loose and floated to the surface, to wash ashore at this point. Holmes studied the thing for a while longer before he spoke.

"This was not designed to fit onto the stump of a severed leg," he said. "Look here, Watson. Note the size and shape of this cavity. I do believe this would accommodate a human knee quite nicely, if the leg were bent double. Indeed, here are a few threads caught in the wood that almost certainly came from a trouser-knee. And look at these extra straps here. They could fit around a leg bent double and hold it in that position."

"Are you saying..?"

"I am saying that our friend Jonathan Small, which is most certainly not his true name, was not a one-legged man at all."

"But why on earth..?"

"I cannot say just yet. Patience, Watson. Just a little more patience."

It was clear that I would need more patience than I believed I possessed. There would be no answers tonight. There was only a hansom cab, Baker Street, and bed.

The next morning, Miss Adler called upon us. Worry was etched into the strong features of her face. I did not need to be Sherlock Holmes to deduce that she had not slept recently.

"There has been no word of Mary, I suppose," she said glumly.

"I fear not," said Holmes.

"What could have happened to her?"

"I have no idea," my friend replied, "but I should like very much to find her. I have a near-complete picture, but the missing components render it worthless."

"Do you think she is dead?" Miss Adler asked anxiously.

Holmes turned his hooded eyes upon her, and spoke sternly. "I believe I just told you that I do not know."

The young lady glared back at him. Only I, who knew Holmes' moods, had detected the slight smile upon his lips and the wry humour in his voice. Perhaps he realized how cruel his remark might have sounded, for he hastened to add:

"That is to say, I cannot know for certain, Miss Adler, but I believe your friend is alive and that we will soon find her."

"Poor little Tonga," said she.

I felt as though an electrical charge had been delivered to me. Glancing at Holmes, I saw that his body had stiffened and his eyes were sharp and glittering.

"What did you call her?" he asked.

"Oh, just a silly childhood nickname," Miss Adler replied dismissively, smiling in spite of her present anguish. "*Tonga* was a dog that belonged to my father. Mary was ever so fond of it."

Holmes and I exchanged a glance. Though he had seemed as shocked as I when Miss Adler had uttered the strange name, there was now something in his expression that suggested he was on firm ground again…just that little hint of self-satisfaction that I had learned to recognize.

"You say the dog belonged to your father," he said to Miss Adler. "Whatever prompted him to select such an unusual name?"

"Well, it belonged to the family, really. I don't... Actually, now that I think of it, Mary named the beast. I don't know where she got it."

"The Tonga," said Holmes, "are an African people, indigenous to southern Zambia, along the Zambezi River. Their name, many scholars believe, comes from a word in the Shona language that means 'independent.'"

"Well, then," said Miss Adler, "it was most fitting, as the hound was *extremely* independent. He simply could not be broken. We kept him for a year, but Tonga was incorrigible. We finally had to get rid of him after he escaped the yard where he had been confined and tried to attack a small child. He had to be put down. Poor Mary was heartbroken. I think she felt a sort of kinship with that rambunctious beast.

"I might as well tell you," she continued gravely, after a lengthy pause, "that Mary was a rather... *troubled* girl. Oh, I said *was*. I must not refer to her in the past tense, so long as there remains the hope that she is still alive."

"Quite right," Holmes said brusquely. "Do please finish what you were about to say. Miss Morstan was... I mean, she *is* a rather troubled girl..?"

Miss Adler nodded.

"Indeed," she said, with just a hint of fire in her eyes and rancor in her voice, "and I put it all down to that father of hers."

"You held a low opinion of Captain Morstan, then?"

"I should say I did...and *still* do. He is a horrid man, and has always neglected Mary shamefully."

"Miss Morstan gave us the impression that she and her father had a most loving relationship," I said.

"Yes, that's Mary," Miss Adler replied. "She idealized him, which was easy to do when he was in India and she did not see him for years. He was a wonderful father so long as he was half a world distant. There were rumors about him. I believe he had some kind of a bad strain in his blood. Though he was born to a good family, he was a natural criminal. Poor Mary's relatives used to speak of him in the most disparaging terms and I do not think the talk was unfounded. I believe that's why Mary's relatives never took to her. They talked openly of some of Arthur Morstan's youthful escapades and hinted that he had not amended his behavior very much as an adult. They said he bought his way into the Army as a means of getting out of the country before he could be charged with some crime or other; perhaps more than one.

"When reality does not suit her, Mary pretends that it is something more palatable. She does not so much lie to others as she does to herself. She knows the things she says are not true, but... Well, I suppose it may have served as the impulse that led her to the stage."

"The stage, you say?" The remark had piqued Holmes' interest.

"Oh, yes, Mary was quite the little actress when we were young. I always thought she could go onstage, but she was very shy about it. She didn't mind school productions, but the idea of appearing before a paying audience of strangers terrified her. A great pity, really. She loved Shakespeare, and liked to essay the more eccentric male roles. It being a girls' school, of course, we had to reverse the traditions of the old Globe Theatre. Mary, in her time, not only played Puck and Caliban, but also Richard the Third, if you can picture that! She twisted herself up into a knot! I swear, she seemed a foot shorter than she actually was; a different person altogether!"

"Had a flair for the dramatic, did she?" Holmes said.

"Under certain circumstances. She could be so timid, and yet there was something wild in her spirit. She often wrote little dramas of her own, which we girls performed for one another. I have to say that they were a

"The stage, you say?"

bit... childish. It was fortunate, I suppose, that she never wanted anyone but us to see them."

Holmes gave me a wordless look that nonetheless conveyed a great deal. One layer of mystery had dropped away from this business. Certain incomprehensibles suddenly made terrible sense.

"She wrote stories too. Silly things, I suppose, all filled with adventure and derring-do. Not the sort of thing one would expect from a girl, but Mary was always something of a tomboy."

"Would you describe her as athletic?" Holmes asked.

"Oh my, yes. She was forever climbing trees and things. And she could run like the wind!"

"Was she a swimmer?"

"Indeed she was—oh, I mean she *is*. I hope... I *hope* she still *is*."

"I think we should have a look through her belongings," Holmes suggested. "We might find something that will give us a clue as to her fate; whatever that might be."

"I am sure Mrs. Forrester would not mind," Miss Adler averred, "under the circumstances. She certainly remembers you fondly."

"Do not give up hope," Holmes advised. "I cannot make promises, but I think that mourning would be very premature."

Mrs. Forrester welcomed Holmes lavishly when we arrived at her home in Lower Camberwell. She was a vivacious woman, and seemed much younger than her two score years. Mister Cecil Forrester had died a few years previously in fact, he was one of the three people Mrs. Forrester had been accused of murdering before Holmes stepped in. Inspector Athelney Jones believed he had made an airtight case against her, based upon his beloved "common sense," but Holmes had swiftly pulled it apart and saved her from the hangman.

Her welcome upon this occasion was so effusive and extravagant that Holmes found himself quite discomfited. I rather enjoyed his efforts to extract himself, especially when the lady insisted on planting kisses on both of his cheeks.

Mrs. Forrester eventually gained control of herself, to Holmes' palpable relief, and led us to Mary Morstan's spartan quarters at the rear of the great house. There wasn't very much to sift through. Mary Morstan had little in the way of material goods. Holmes did find, underneath the bed, the small cask which contained the pearls, and Holmes entrusted it to Miss Adler.

"Keep them safe," he said, "for your friend will be glad to have them when we find her." Holmes was still down upon his hands and knees, and he said, "Hello, there seems to be something else under here. Ah, yes, now this might tell us something."

It was an old note-book, of the kind a schoolgirl might possess. Holmes flipped it open and nodded. He held it so I could see that several pages had been torn from it. Holmes examined the thing briefly, then handed it to me.

On the front cover, I saw, inscribed in chillingly familiar block print, the words "Property of Mary Minerva Morstan."

"Minerva?" I wondered aloud.

"Oh, her middle name is really Clara," said Miss Adler. "She was forever putting on little airs like that, just for sport."

"Sport indeed," said Holmes. "Tell me, has Miss Morstan always been troubled by severe headaches?"

"Yes she has, ever since she was very young. She has seen a slew of doctors. Specialists, you know. They tell her it is all in her head, which it *is*, of course, but not in the way they mean."

"This places a rather different complexion on the matter," said Holmes.

I simply shook my head; unable to rationalize what I knew must be the truth. The thing was both crystal-clear and utterly opaque at the same time. I did not dare even try to draw any conclusions.

"Well, I think I know all that I need to know in order to bring this matter to a close," said Holmes. "I must make some preparations today, and I think tomorrow will see an end to it."

CHAPTER FIFTEEN
Small Returns

y 8 o'clock the following evening, Holmes had made his preparations, and there was nothing left to do but await developments. I knew most of what he had done, and I still had my doubts but Holmes seemed to have none, so I held my tongue. He had allowed me a small glimpse behind the veil of mystery, but insisted on leaving the thing in place until his scheme could be played out.

At 8:15, we heard the bell downstairs. Holmes became instantly alert. Mrs. Hudson gone out for the evening, at Holmes' insistence, and the door was answered by a substitute of whom more anon.

Doctor Doyle arrived at our door unannounced. Holmes was about to send him on his way when the bell downstairs rang again.

"Too late now," he said. "Just have a seat, Doctor. You may bear witness to the denouement. Just be still and do not fret over anything that happens. It may appear dire, but I have taken extraordinary precautions."

"Come in," Holmes called out. "It is not locked."

The door swung open and in stepped our recent adversary, the abominable Jonathan Small. He had arrived, I noticed with some relief, by himself. He also held in his hand a revolver, which was no relief at all.

"Mister *Small*," Holmes said mockingly. "May I offer you something to drink?"

"Please, Holmes," said our visitor with a sickening grin, "you know I am not your guest. You know why I am here, what I have come to do."

"You seem to have grown a new leg," Holmes remarked. "That is perhaps the most remarkable thing I have ever seen. Certain lizards are able to re-grow their tails, but I have never before..."

"Mister Holmes, please. Is this the way you wish to end your life, with buffoonery? It's up to you, of course, but it belies your formidable reputation. Don't you want to know the truth about this whole business?"

"I already do," said Holmes. "You can tell me nothing. I saw you take what might have been a fatal plunge into the river, but of course it was nothing of the sort."

"I am an excellent swimmer," said he.

"Where is your small companion, *Small*?"

"Tonga is dead."

"How certain are you of that? Perhaps Tonga is an excellent swimmer too."

The man hesitated before answering. "I am as certain as I can be. But it is none of your concern. Nothing is, as of this moment."

"That's really quite clever," Holmes said, patting his hands together in mock applause. "You have a way with threats."

"I also have a way of carrying them out. So you know everything, do you?"

"I know there was never a Jonathan Small. We found your wooden leg on the embankment, you see. I knew that you had survived, because that elaborate web of leather straps did not loosen itself to escape from your dead body. You removed it and swam away. But I knew you were a fraud long before that. I found your foot-prints all over town. A man with a peg-leg presumably knows how to walk as naturally as possible upon it. Whoever made those tracks did not. The supposed peg-prints were not of a uniform depth, as were the shoe-prints. The depth varied widely, and the shape as well, as though it had skidded about. Were you aware of that discrepancy, *Mister Sholto*?"

The man nodded. "You know who I am, then…Bartholomew Sholto."

With his free hand, our sinister visitor removed a false beard and a wig, and wiped some of the dark make-up from his face.

He was both familiar to me, and utterly alien.

This individual was the image of Thaddeus Sholto in every way, though he could hardly have been more different. It was in the way he carried himself and the deeply malevolent look in his eyes. A shudder passed through me as his gaze briefly caught mine. In that moment, I understood perfectly what Mrs. Smith had said to us.

"If you know anything of me," he said to Holmes, "you know that I am a rather dangerous man. My brother thinks that I have some good in me, but he is mistaken. You know what I have done, and I am afraid that the knowledge must die with you."

"A question first, if you please," Holmes said calmly. "Did you kill the Grand Duke in order to sabotage certain negotiations? You must have collected all manner of interesting information while you were a blackmailer."

"I work for no one save myself. I may accept a commission now and again, if it is profitable enough."

"That is not an answer."

"It is the only one that you shall have. You may infer from it what you will."

"Well, Mister Sholto. I daresay that in exposing you, I will have helped remove a plague spot from the West End of London."

"You speak as though you had some control over the situation, Holmes."

"Oh, I *do*," my friend replied. "You see, I took the liberty of issuing an invitation to a prominent member of the detective force. He has concealed himself on the landing outside my door. We've been waiting for you, and now the game is up. Jones! If you would, please!"

The door swung open and in stepped Athelney Jones. I held my breath.

The police inspector gazed upon the three seated occupants of the room with a queer expression on his face. "Why haven't you killed them?" he asked Sholto. "What the devil are you waiting for?"

"You, Jones. You know more about me and my activities than I do about you and yours. I know enough to make you uncomfortable, but what if the criminal charges couldn't be made to stick? It has been many years, and you've had plenty of time to make arrangements in case anyone became suspicious. I want you to murder Mister Holmes, Doctor Watson, and this other fellow. That, I think, will restore a sense of balance."

Jones puffed out his cheeks and scratched his head.

"Very well," he said. "It will be to my advantage to have them removed from the field, that much is certain. I swear that Holmes is positively uncanny. He gives me the whim-whams at times."

"I am in league with the devil," said Holmes. "I have strange, mystical powers. You cannot make a move, Jones, that I am not aware of. You accepted the blackmail money from Oscar Wilde, did you not? Yes, I know *everything*, Jones."

"What is this about Oscar Wilde?" Sholto asked angrily.

Jones seemed quite unnerved, and I wondered what he thought of Holmes' remarks. Perspiration stood out on his brow and his lips twitched.

"That is all very well, Holmes," said he, ignoring Sholto's query. "But your clairvoyance failed you, did it not, when you called upon me to come arrest Sholto! You are lying. You never suspected me of anything. Admit it. I never did anything to Oscar Wilde. He's lying, Sholto, making things up."

"For God's sake, just kill them," Sholto urged.

"I see all and know all," said Holmes. "Your doom is written, Jones."

"Have you any last words?" Jones asked with a sadistic grin on his face that did not quite cancel out the superstitious fear in his eyes.

"I have words," Holmes said calmly, "but I hardly think they will be my last. Here they are: *Have you heard enough, Lestrade?*"

"Indeed I have, sir, and then some."

The curtain at the back of the room swept aside, and out stepped Lestrade, pistol in hand. Beside him was a very large uniformed constable.

Jones whirled around and leveled his pistol at Lestrade, but the young constable was much too swift. Before Jones knew what had happened, the constable had snatched his gun away and knocked him to the floor.

"By God, that felt good," said he. "Nothing I hate worse than a bent copper."

Lestrade clapped him on the shoulder. "Excellent work, Collins."

"I wouldn't mind hitting him again, sir."

"Perhaps later, Collins. For now, just get the bracelets on him if you'd be so kind."

As for Sholto, he had remained motionless, seemingly dumbstruck, as Jones had been taken down. Doyle and I had gotten to our feet and come around behind him, and now each of us held one of his arms. Holmes relieved him of his pistol, and passed it to Lestrade.

"You see, Jones," Holmes said, "you were not the only member of the detective force I took the liberty of inviting here. Lestrade got here first."

"That is all well and good, Holmes," Jones said. "But how will you prove anything against me?"

"Oh, I have my ways. You speak almost as if you had a leg to stand on, Jones! If we cannot make a charge of attempted murder stick, there is a great deal more to choose from. I've two other guests here this evening that you might like to meet. Oscar, would you just step in here please?"

Another door opened, and into the room stepped Oscar Wilde, attired in a deerstalker cap and an Inverness cape. And he was not alone. With him, on a lead, was the dog Toby.

"Good evening, sir," Wilde said to Jones. "Do you like my outfit?"

Jones stood silent. Lestrade spoke up:

"He must do. The outfit was found in his rooms, along with a few other interesting items. Oh, don't look so shocked, Jones. I have been on to you for some time."

Meanwhile, Toby, straining at his lead, had approached Jones and was poking his furry snout into the disgraced inspector's jacket.

"Get this beast away from me," Jones snarled, twisting from side to side in Collins' firm grip.

"What do you have in there, Jones?" Holmes asked. "Shall we just have a look? Ah, your pocket-book. Quite a few bank-notes in it, I see. They are what drew Toby's attention. You see, some of these notes have been smeared with a minute quantity of creosote, a substance for which Toby has a fondness. I took the liberty of treating the currency that was handed over to a blackmailer who wore the same garments Oscar is wearing now; the ones that were discovered in your home by Lestrade and his men."

"Pah!" Jones scoffed, though he looked troubled. "Such evidence will never stand up in court."

"Perhaps, perhaps not," said Lestrade. "But I think the attempted mur-der of Sherlock Holmes, Doctor Watson and Doctor Doyle will do for the time being. I am quite sure that abundant evidence of your other misdeeds will surface in short order. For example, I understand that you might soon find yourself up on a charge of arson, in connection with a fire at a certain gentlemen's club in Pall Mall.

"I arrest you in the Queen's name as being concerned in the attempted murders of three men. It is my duty to inform you that anything which you may say will be used against you…but you know all about that, do you not? And, of course, the same goes for you Sholto…"

As Lestrade spoke his name, Sholto suddenly twisted his arms and broke away from Doyle and myself. Quick as a flash, he reached the window and flung it open. He had jumped up onto the sill as nimbly as a hare, and was preparing to leap to the street below, when the flat crack of a shot rang out and a bullet caught him in the shoulder. He fell back into the room with a groan.

"That would be Sacker," said Lestrade, in a self-satisfied manner. "One of the best sharpshooters on the force. Mister Holmes suggested that we put him up temporarily in the empty house across the street, just in case we had another Jefferson Hope on our hands."

Lestrade referred to an incident that had taken place in our rooms some four years previously, during the investigation of the murder of Enoch Drebber. A man named Jefferson Hope had attempted to escape from police custody by leaping through the very window Sholto had just tried to utilize.

"And," came a voice from behind us, "had he used the stairs, he'd have received much the same treatment."

Miss Adler had ascended the stairs and stood framed in the doorway. Her maid's costume was incongruous upon her, but no more so than the trim revolver she held in her right hand. There was something strangely fetching about her at that moment, and I wondered if Holmes recognized it as I did. It certainly was not lost on Doyle, as he later confided to me.

I examined Sholto's wound, which was very minor; the bullet had buried itself in the fleshy part of his shoulder. I placed a compress over it. "He is in no danger," said I. "Except perhaps from the hangman."

Two more constables had joined us in our sitting-room, having materialized from I knew not where.

"Holland," Lestrade said, "you and Sallis help this young gentleman downstairs. Our doctor will have a look at him once he's locked up."

Jones was, perhaps, a pitiable figure, but I felt no pity for him, and it was quite plain that Holmes did not.

"You are a disgrace to virtually everything to which you have any connection," he said coldly. "The police force, certainly. Your family, without doubt. The human race itself, arguably. Know this, Athelney Jones: You are not a clever man, and you are certainly not a criminal mastermind. You had great and undeserved good fortune which has allowed you to conceal your part in your crimes for so many years. But that has been stripped away from you now. I was the agent by which this was accomplished, but your ruin is entirely your own doing.

"You went off on your own, did you not, when you decided to blackmail Oscar Wilde? I thought it rather strange that a West End blackmailer would instruct his victim to meet him on the edge of Whitechapel. It did not fit in with everything else I knew, but Lestrade kindly cleared the matter up for me."

"When he was just a young constable," said Lestrade, "Jones used to walk a beat in Whitechapel. He knows every inch of the place, I'd wager."

"You are not directly guilty of any capital crimes, Jones," Holmes continued, inexorably, "and you are in reasonably good health. It would be a great pity if you did not live to see a ripe old age whilst you are detained at Her Majesty's pleasure."

"One hates to see a brother officer, as it were, bring disgrace upon himself in this way," said Lestrade. "How could you do it, Jones?"

"Oh, shut your hole, Lestrade," Jones snarled. "Butter wouldn't melt in your mouth, would it? Pious jackass! If I weren't restrained, I'd give you a good thrashing."

"Indeed," said Lestrade with a smile, "and if my dear old Aunt Sophia were equipped with wheels, she'd be a wagon. I'm almost tempted to have Collins remove those bracelets and let you have a go. But I'm afraid I might do too much damage. We'll want you in fit enough shape to stand in the dock, after all. That's just *common sense*, isn't it, Athelney?"

"I shall tell what I know, Mister Sherlock Holmes," vowed Jones. "Pretty sorts of clients you have! I'll tell what I know about that girl and everything else as well. That holier-than-thou brother of yours... You've not heard the last of me! I'll give evidence against Sholto too. You will all suffer for the things I know."

"Collins," said Lestrade, "take this creature out of my sight, there's a good lad. Get him down to the nearest sub-station. I'll be along directly."

The constable nodded smartly and led Athelney Jones away. I, for one, was glad to see the back of him.

"Jones was correct about this cap," said Lestrade. "It would never hold up as evidence of anything in court. I doubt that he will ever be tried for blackmailing Mister Wilde, though I shall make every effort to retrieve the money he took. You might as well keep the hat as a memento, Mister Holmes. The cape too."

My friend looked upon the proffered garments with distaste.

"I have never worn such an ensemble in my life," he said. "I am hardly a country squire."

"No one is suggesting that you wear them," said I. "But they will make rather nice trophies, don't you think?"

"Oh, you'd cut a very dashing figure in these togs," said Wilde. "Hunting clothes to befit a great manhunter. It is aesthetically correct, Holmes. You simply *must*."

"I would look like a fool, parading about town in them," Holmes said. "They would stand out. Stalking deer in the forest is one thing; stalking men in a city is quite another."

"Well, give it some thought, anyhow," said Wilde.

Before Lestrade left, he took Wilde aside and said, "Er, Mister Wilde, do you suppose I might, er, trouble you for your autograph? It's for my wife, of course."

"How did you know when Sholto would come here?" I demanded of Holmes after Lestrade had departed. "You must have had some idea when you asked Jones to station himself on the landing."

"You have it backward, Watson. My invitation to Jones made it certain that Sholto would come while he was stationed here. I told Jones that I *had information* that the culprit was going to show up at a particular time. Jones, of course, conveyed this to Sholto, who contrived to appear at the proper hour. The prospect of catching me so flat-footed was irresistible; a killer in league with the police officer I believed was going to arrest him! What could be neater, and what could be more of a slap in the face to the smug and superior Mister Sherlock Holmes? So caught up in it were they that neither of them thought to question the nature of the information I thought I had or its source."

"Masterful," Doyle proclaimed it, and I agreed.

Something occurred to me then. "But where is Thaddeus? My God, Holmes, do you think he has been disposed of?"

"Well, in a manner of speaking, perhaps."

"That makes no sense, Holmes."

"I trust that it will before too much longer, Watson. I believe I know where we will find the answers we seek. It should be safe enough now, and you have been patient long enough. Would you care to make one final trip with me to Pondicherry?"

"Shall I accompany you?" Doyle asked.

"I think not. I do not anticipate any danger, but one can never know for sure. I have played some risky games of late, and it is just good fortune that there have been so few deaths. Watson. you will, it goes without saying, accompany me, and bring your service revolver with you."

The great brooding house was closed up. Every window was dark. We did not bother knocking at the front door. Holmes led me around to the rear, where he produced a set of lockpicks and went to work on the door. Within a very few moments we were inside.

As we moved through the dark ground floor rooms toward the staircase, I was struck by how the atmosphere of the place seemed to have changed since last I was there. Everything was the same, yet strangely different. The air of oppression I had experienced was absent now.

We went up the staircase, to the first floor, the former domain of Bartholomew Sholto. I saw the "fence" that Holmes had spoken of. The door set into it stood open.

It was eerily quiet as we made our way down the dark hallway. From around the corner at the end of the corridor came a feeble light.

As we rounded the corner, we saw, in the flickering light of a lantern, a small figure, huddled against the wall next to a great oaken door.

"Miss Morstan," Holmes said gently. "It is over."

CHAPTER SIXTEEN
The Truth

"Oh, thank God that you are all right," she cried, rushing to me. She placed her hands upon my face and smiled through her tears. I was terribly glad to see her, alive and well, if in some distress. I comforted her as best I could.

"Our friend 'Mister Small' survived his plunge into the Thames," said Holmes. "He came to Baker Street and made a final attempt to salvage his situation, but matters took a turn that he had not anticipated. He is safely in custody now, and will stand trial for his crimes."

"And I suppose I shall have to do the same," Miss Morstan said.

"We can discuss that later."

"I do not understand," said I, for I did not.

"Just a little more patience, Watson," said Holmes. "We are almost there." He touched the door. "Is he here, Miss Morstan?"

"Yes," said she, "I came to see him, but he will not admit me to his room."

Holmes knocked upon the door with his knuckles. "Mister Bartholomew Sholto!" he said in an authoritative tone. "This is Sherlock Holmes. I am here with Doctor Watson and Miss Morstan."

I looked at him. "*Bartholomew* Sholto? How can it be?"

Holmes silenced me with a wave of his hand. "Sholto!" he rapped. "You've nothing to fear. I know everything now, or near enough. Your brother has been arrested, and I shall see to it that the authorities know the truth. You are in no danger."

The door slowly opened. Standing before us was the very image of Thaddeus Sholto...but for one ghastly difference.

"Oh!" Mary Morstan exclaimed, "what have you done to your poor face?"

The entire left side was hideously reddened, as though it had been burned, and disfigured by long, thin lacerations that had barely begun to heal. Whatever he had done, he had done it very recently and very thoroughly. It was clear to me that he would be disfigured for life.

"What I should have done long ago," said he, in a bleak tone. "I fear that I have facilitated my brother's wrongdoing by providing him with such an easy scapegoat. Now, everyone will be able to tell us apart."

"You must allow me to treat that," said I. The man waved me away.

"I would prefer that you did not," he said grimly. His voice was light but rich, and would have been quite beautiful, had it not been shot through with suffering and bitterness. "It is the only bold statement I have ever made in my life. Let it be."

"This, Watson, is *Bartholomew* Sholto," said Holmes. "It was Mister Thaddeus that we apprehended in Baker Street. We have been intentionally misled as to his own character and that of his brother. Mister Sholto, we should like very much to hear your story from your own lips. Your brother will not interfere with you ever again, if that is your wish."

Bartholomew did not seem pleased. His countenance, even apart from the horrible damage he had wrought upon it, was downcast and depressed. He struck me as a man who had never known happiness.

He stood aside and let us pass into the room, a cold, barely-furnished chamber. We took seats upon the mismatched chairs. Illuminated by the flickering light of a dozen candles, we listened to what this strange young man had to say.

"Our father was a scoundrel," said Bartholomew Sholto, "as was Miss Morstan's. I am sorry to say it, but there it is. They were thick as thieves, and I mean that quite literally, when they were young. As the years passed, they grew older but never grew up. The two of them schemed together in India. They both shamefully abused their positions, and were cautioned more than once by Lord Northbrook himself. But nothing could be proved against them.

"And it was they who robbed the Hallward establishment in 1877 and that was the source of their 'treasure.' Father and Colonel Morstan took a leave from their duties in India and participated in the robbery. Thaddeus had planned it out for them. I had already had a long and wearisome experience of their shenanigans. I learned of this latest outrage and, in a moment of passion, cast aside my usual practices and informed the police.

"Father and Arthur Morstan got away, but Thaddeus was apprehended along with a hired man. My brother told them he was me, as was his custom since childhood whenever he was caught out. He was released on bail and I took his place at trial."

"How did he force you into that?" I asked.

"He did not," said Bartholomew in a hollow voice, staring at the wall in front of him and through it, seeing God knows what. "I took his place willingly. I had done the same sort of thing before, many times, going back to our schoolboy days. I was not worried about myself, you see, but I knew that Thad was in danger of losing his soul. I thought he could be saved. Always, he was a devil, and so I tried to be an angel. For so many years, I tried to save him. I see how foolish it was, now that everything has come undone."

"When Thaddeus was apprehended," said Holmes, "it was a simple matter for him to arrange things so that Bartholomew went to prison. He had spent years blackening his brother's reputation, so it was quite plausible. He simply claimed that he *was* Bartholomew. When he was released on bail pending his trial, the brothers switched places."

"When I was released from prison," Bartholomew took up the narrative, "it was already too late for my father…he was dead, and gone to his final judgment…but I thought I could still save Thad. I bided my time and kept a close eye on him. Eventually, I found out what had become of the stolen loot. It was not at the bottom of the Thames. Father had arranged the whole thing, and he kept the gold for himself. To his dying day, Morstan believed that the proceeds of the robbery were lost."

"That is where Athelney Jones came in," said Holmes. "He was the only witness to the 'loss' of the loot."

Sholto nodded. "Which of course was never lost. It was a sham, a design of my father's to fool his friend, Morstan. Jones worked out the truth on the spot, and he recognized my father. He said nothing to his superiors, but approached Father shortly after with what he knew. He accepted money for his silence, and he did even more than that. He joined my father and my brother, in a variety of criminal escapades. He was their 'inside man' at Scotland Yard.

"But back to the robbery. Father and Thad hadn't dared to cash in the gold through any legitimate agency. They traded it off to a dealer in stolen goods, who would have it melted and recast in various forms. In return, he gave them cash, a variety of precious stones, and a cask filled with very fine pearls. Small things, and easier to hide, but quite precious.

"Miss Morstan's father came to London again in 1878. I do not know why, but I imagine that he suspected our father of some skullduggery with regard to the 'lost' loot. I do not know exactly what passed between them, as I was in prison at the time, but I am quite certain that either Father or Thaddeus, or the two of them acting in concert, murdered him. Perhaps you can get the truth out of Thad.

"After *our* Father's death, and my return from prison, Thad ran through the cash rather quickly, but kept the stones and pearls hidden away. It took me some time to discover the truth, bit by bit, about the aftermath of the robbery and the disposition of the loot. And I might never have discovered their hiding-place had he not run short on funds and begun to dip into his treasure trove. This was shortly before he came up with his... new sideline.

"The pearls were stolen property, albeit a generation removed, as it were, but I felt that Miss Morstan had been wronged, by her own father as well as my own, and I believe there is a higher law than man's. So I began filching pearls and sending them to her.

"When Thad inevitably learned what I had been doing, as he did this year, his first thought was to kill Miss Morstan. I did not learn of this until after you gentlemen had thwarted his attempt. For that, I am most grateful to you.

"Thad also moved his 'treasure' to a new hiding place, but he was not very clever about it. Oh, he was cunning enough, but he couldn't fool me. I discovered it immediately and moved it yet again, which placed him in an uncomfortable position, to say the least.

"Of course, he knew that I had done it, and he cursed himself for his carelessness. He never confronted me directly, for that was never his way. He let me know that he knew, and he made many a veiled threat. But he did not dare do anything to me, for he believed he might need me again. He had grown accustomed to his scapegoat, and he could not bear to do without me.

"I suppose he didn't think it was very important. He knew I would not dispose of it entirely, and he could afford to wait, since he now had a profitable little business.

"Over the years, he had made a great many sinister acquaintances, and together with a small band of them, he set up his blackmailing business. It was made to order for a man like Thaddeus; a social butterfly, sought after by the wealthy and well-known and utterly without conscience.

"Shortly after the attempt on Miss Morstan, I realized what a dangerous game I had been playing. I wrestled with it in my heart and soul, and finally I resolved to hand him over to the police. But then...before I could do that..." He faltered and cast his eyes down to the floor.

"I approached Thaddeus Sholto," said Mary Morstan firmly

I was quite shocked by this. Holmes, it was evident, was not.

"I thought he must not be quite what he seemed because of that book I saw in his house," she went on. "There was something horrible about it, and yet... compelling at the same time. And I was certain that Thaddeus knew something of my father's fate, so I went to his house and confronted him directly. At first he feigned ignorance, but when he saw how determined I was, he relented. Or so I thought.

"He told me about the robbery and that both his father and mine were dead. He also told me that he had not been involved in any of it...it was all down to Bartholomew, he claimed. He told me that he had discovered where the hoard was hidden and had been sending the pearls to me, but that Bartholomew had discovered what he was doing, moved the valuables to a new hiding-place, and tried to have me murdered.

"Well, I gave him to understand that I cared nothing for the law, and did not care about any criminal activities in which his brother might have been involved. Which was true at the time, I'm afraid. All I wanted was a small share of the loot, I said, and I would never cause trouble for either of them if I received it.

"But he was concerned, as was I, that Sherlock Holmes might uncover the true story. I had not been able to resist Irene's demand that we consult with him, and now he was well and truly in it. And so Thaddeus and I came up with the tale of the Agra treasure and Jonathan Small. That was mostly my work. I thought it was plausible enough, and impossible to disprove."

"You should have known Holmes would not be taken in for long by such a tale," I said. "Whyever did you take such a risk?"

"I did not know what else to do. I wished I hadn't allowed Irene to talk me into engaging Mister Holmes, but realized that, if I had not, I would likely be dead. So, *that* had been for the best, and I convinced myself that the situation could still be salvaged.

"Thaddeus assured me that Mister Holmes would not be a problem for us. He might be tricked into helping us locate the hidden loot, and then..."

"And then *what*, Miss?" Holmes asked gently.

"He...well, he said that you were a sort of mercenary, after all. You weren't a member of the police force, you did what you did as a free agent, to earn your keep, and that your silence could be purchased."

"Did you believe that was what he intended?"

"I...I convinced myself that I did. All that concerned me was the 'treasure.' I thought it was mine by right, and see where it has brought me. By helping Thaddeus I thought I was...oh, I don't know. I knew it was wrong, and that is the thing I cannot get around. I wanted lots of money. I see now what a sad, empty ambition that is.

"He seemed such a good man at first, and I believed that the evil in that house was the work of his brother. Thaddeus was incredibly charming; almost angelic in a way. Until one discovered his bad side, which I soon would. He drew me into his world. I did not know at first how twisted a soul he had. And before I realized it, my own soul had begun to distort itself. Our plan, it seems to me now, was mad. But at the time I was under the influence of not only Thaddeus Sholto, but also the opium he persuaded me to sample with him. That made everything so much easier."

"Yes," Holmes said. "I have tried it myself, and found that the effect it produced was the opposite of what I sought. It was pleasant enough, but I was not interested in pleasure. I wanted sharpness and immediacy, not self-satisfied torpor."

"Torpor, it seemed, was what I craved. It was insidious and wonderful all at once. Things which had always mattered no longer did, and vice versa. We concocted our little charade. Wherever the treasure might be, Sherlock Holmes could surely find it. That was what I thought. That was all I wanted. I didn't know it was all just a game to Thaddeus. And he enjoyed it…manipulating you, I mean. And me.

"But before we could go to work on you, Mister Holmes, Thad told me that a problem had arisen. The Grand Duke was being blackmailed by Bartholomew and might cause disaster in the household. If all of the truth came out, we should never have our money. We would have to scare him off. A very unlikely scenario, perhaps, but I was not thinking at all clearly.

"To be honest, I don't believe Thaddeus is entirely sane and I *know* that *I* am not."

"What do you mean by that?" Holmes asked.

"I have pains in my head, and sometimes my thoughts seem not to be my own. Out of the blue, I become angry and wish to do ill. Other times, I experience a pervasive euphoria. At times I believe in the most outlandish ideas, and regard every-day realities as bizarre impossibilities.

"But, you see, the opium made me feel more… *normal*, I suppose. That is to say, it twisted my conscious mind to the point where my strange fancies seemed quite logical.

"By this time, we had worked out our story, which involved the fictional Jonathan Small and Tonga, and we decided to play the characters. Thaddeus told me that we were going to deliver a scare to the Grand Duke, and that it would be a good situation in which to try out our new identities, should it be necessary for them to put in an appearance later on.

"He provided me with those thorns. We confronted his highness through the window of that house and made some extravagant threats. He laughed at us and sat down at that table. Before we took our leave, I put the thorn into him, using the blow-pipe. Thaddeus told me that the thorns were dipped in a soporific, and that it would scare the Grand Duke into submission. That...wasn't true, was it, Mister Holmes?"

"I'm afraid it was not," Holmes said.

"It was poison, wasn't it?"

"Yes. But you did not know."

"That does no good to the men I...murdered. And I should have known. I was either mad or willfully blind or both."

"You may have behaved foolishly, but you are not a killer."

"Not deliberately. Does that make any difference, really?"

"It does in the eyes of the law," Holmes declared. "If you cannot see it, that is to your credit, but you must accept what has happened and how you were led into it. You must not condemn yourself when no one around you is doing so. But pray continue your narrative."

"Very well. When you showed up with Mister Wilde and offered to paint Thaddeus' portrait, he began to think that things would be all right after all. He could keep you close and perhaps learn what you knew or thought you knew. You might even discover Bart's hiding place if you were given the run of the house. It was then that we decided to go ahead with our story. I suggested to you that we visit Thad and ask him what he knew. This would work in conjunction with our Small and Tonga personae. Within a few days, we would present the last act, after paving the way with the 'Testament.' To begin it, he gave you the tale we had prepared about our fathers' deaths."

"That was where you—or rather Thaddeus—made a capital mistake," Holmes said.

"Yes. It didn't seem suspicious at first, since I knew the whole thing was a sham. That he would be confused about certain elements seemed plausible enough. But it made me think. My infatuation with him was beginning to wear thin. The spell he had cast over me at the beginning had begun to fade, and I was seeing the man inside.

"At any rate, we played out our charade, then I returned to your rooms the next day, as myself, where I learned that the man Davies had been located, and also that our little hideout was being watched. Both held alarming possibilities, and I went directly back to Thaddeus.

"Thaddeus had owned the little house for many years. He liked to go there, disguise himself, and move among the people of that district. His reasons for doing so, I later learned, were utterly vile.

"You must accept what has happened and how you were led into it."

"He told me Davies would be a problem, and that we would have to 'throw a scare into him,' as we had done with the Grand Duke. I hoped we could get there before you did. Well, you know how that turned out. I could no longer deny Thaddeus' true nature, and I could no longer pretend that I meant well…not if I continued on my course.

"That was when I knew I must confront Bartholomew.

"You see, Mister Holmes, I had been thinking about what you said about Bartholomew Sholto's cunning nature. You said that he would not hide the treasure in his own living quarters, because that would be the first place Thaddeus would look if he could manage to. It occurred to me that Bartholomew might in fact be *so* cunning that he would anticipate this deduction on someone's part and hide the treasure in his private domain after all.

"It seemed worth looking into, so I did. I did not gain entrance to the upper floors through the interior of the house. I scaled a large tree in the back garden and got onto the roof. Slowly and carefully, I made a hole. It took me several hours to do the work in complete or near-complete silence.

"Finally, I broke through and found myself in Bartholomew Sholto's sanctum, and I discovered a sensitive soul rather than the fearsome creature his brother had spoken of. I told him all that I knew, he told me all that he knew. He told me the *truth,* and we reached an accord.

"As it happened, you were correct, Mister Holmes. The treasure was indeed secreted elsewhere in the house. But now that both you and Thaddeus would be searching for it, Bart and I decided that it should be moved. Taking a leaf from your book, I thought about the very last place Thaddeus would think to look for it. It was quite simple; Bart took it to the waterfront house Thaddeus was using for our transformations into 'Jonathan Small' and 'Tonga.'

"Bart had won me over to his side, but I was still in a quandary. I was afraid of what Thaddeus might do if I openly defied him.

"And my fears were well-founded, for he *did* discover what Bart and I had done. How, I do not know. Thaddeus threatened to kill his brother if I did not lead him to the loot. He did not expressly threaten to kill *me*, but I thought it was implied.

"How foolish I had been! But I still thought I could salvage the situation without losing my life *or* tarnishing my own reputation. I told him that we must close the thing out, and that he could not do this without me. We would play the last act and consign Jonathan Small and Tonga to the bottom of the Thames, along with the fictional treasure.

"I thought long and hard about how I could use the information I had, and keep it a secret from Thaddeus. Then it struck me. The proper course was not to *conceal*, but to *reveal*. I told him about the boys there on watch, then carefully suggested my plan.

"I told him again that the only thing I was interested in was the loot, and that I cared nothing for Bart or for him. That was something he could understand, and it became the basis for what followed. He 'trusted' me once again, because he believed I was acting in my own best interest. I told him that I would help him throw you off his trail for good, in return for half of the loot.

"With that in mind, I finished the Testament and had it delivered to you. The thing was based upon a story I wrote when I was still a young girl; an epic melodrama in which my father played the hero. I never finished it back then, but when this business arose, I remembered it.

"Once that produced the desired effect, Thad and I could go to the building and I would give him the treasure. I convinced him that we should make use of the little steam launch he owned. We would wait until we could be sure you were near, then make a break for the boat and appear to be escaping down the river. At some point, we would make it appear as though the both of us had gone overboard with the loot. Jonathan Small and Tonga would be dead, and the loot lost forever; so far as everyone else was concerned. That was the plan that I presented to Thaddeus. Of course, I had something quite different in mind.

"Once we arrived at the house, we dithered around until your boys had time to get word to Baker Street and bring you to the scene. Thaddeus had the boat ready.

"I wanted you to catch Thaddeus with the loot in his possession, if possible, because I also knew that once it was all over, he might very well kill me if he went free.

"I got on the boat with him, planning to incapacitate him at some point. He did not know that the man Smith had his steam launch ready for you, but it actually seemed to be a blessing for us. You would witness the denouement at close quarters. It was intended that we, as Small and Tonga, should go overboard and be presumed dead. That is what Thaddeus believed, and he provided breathing-tubes for the both of us. I discovered later that my tube had been plugged up. It is good that I am a strong swimmer, and no stranger to holding my breath for long periods.

"I knew, of course, that *you* would know the truth about me, but how could you prove anything?

"In the testament, I gave you the best clues that I could as to what was going on and what our plans were. I knew that you were aware of the earlier robbery, and what had supposedly happened to the stolen property.

"I wanted the loot to be found and taken away from Thaddeus, and somehow used to compensate the victims of the original robbery. I would keep back only as much as I would need to take myself far from England. But when I saw Thaddeus about to murder Doctor Watson, I lost my head and used the first thing at hand as a weapon; the cask full of jewels and pearls! I never even gave it a second thought.

"Well, I would simply have to bear the loss of it. I could reappear as myself later on, no one would know that Tonga and I were one and the same, and all would be right with my world! I would have lost nothing, after all and I still had my pearls. If Thaddeus survived and told of my involvement, my hope was that his story would not be believed. Who would take seriously the notion that I was that strange savage creature?"

She fell silent at that point, and closed her eyes. I thought I perceived great relief on her face and in her bearing. She seemed almost carefree.

"What did you mean earlier, Holmes, when you spoke of the capital mistake Thaddeus made?" I asked.

"Remember," said Holmes, "what Thaddeus told us about his father's death: that he and his brother were present. And remember that he *also* told us that Major Sholto died shortly before Bartholomew Sholto was released from prison. *Il faut bonne mémoire après qu'on a menti.*

"Of course, it might have been an innocent mistake. He could have been wrong about one circumstance, but not the other. I had a look at the prison records, and found that Bartholomew was not released until *after* the Major's death; there can be no doubt of that. Thus, his story surrounding the Major's deathbed remarks was a fabrication.

"And so, imagine the effect it had on me when I saw that selfsame error repeated in the Testament! It was a message, of course, a message from *you*, Miss Morstan. It had to be deliberate. With that in hand, I reevaluated the document and found the other clues you left."

She opened her eyes and nodded, the expression on her delicate features almost beatific there in the candlelight. "I included the Grand Duke in the story of the treasure scheme not to throw you off, but as a sign to point you to the truth. That he could have been involved at all was such an absurd notion..."

"Yes," said Holmes. "It was difficult to miss the fact that he had been clumsily appended to the tale. Thaddeus Sholto might have let it pass, but

I could not. You are really to be commended. You were working both with me and against me, and you did a remarkable job. But when you turned up later, after the supposed death of Tonga, you must have known that I would know."

"Knowing and proving are two entirely different things, Mister Holmes."

Holmes laughed and clapped his hands together. "Capital!" he exclaimed. "You are a most remarkable young woman. A worthy friend *and* foe all at once!"

"And, of course," Miss Morstan continued, "you are not a police official. I sensed that you were a man confident enough in himself to follow dictates from a higher source. I would be out of it, I thought, and I could go somewhere far away." She shook her head, and tears slid down her cheeks."How can I be such a fool?"

"If you had just told me the truth when you learned it from Bartholomew," said Holmes, "this elaborate charade would not have been necessary. Why, then, am I so pleased that you did not? Why do I have the feeling that you have, in some strange way, saved me from something I cannot name?"

He suddenly became serious. "If it were within my power to keep the police from knowing the role you played," he said gravely, "I would do so. To be frank, once I became aware of what you were endeavoring to do, I hoped that you would get away with it. You had a number of pernicious influences at work upon you. But it is out of my hands now. Thaddeus might not be believed, but Athelney Jones will tell them all about it, if only for spite. There is no way to prevent it. Indeed, he may have done so already.

"However, we may place the blame for the killings where it belongs; with Thaddeus Sholto. I find it admirable that you are willing to accept the consequences of your actions, but there is no need to overdo it.

"Thaddeus will continue to insist that he is his brother. He is a resourceful man, and will no doubt have some plan in place to break out of custody. Once he does that, he is free to resume his existence as the poor, innocent Sholto brother, and Bartholomew will take the blame for his wrongdoing as per usual. Or so he believes."

Bartholomew Sholto, who had been sitting silent, as though in some kind of stupor, spoke once again: "It is over at last. Since my brother is in custody, it is time to bring all of this to an end. He will never change, and I will not suffer again for his wrongdoing. The scales have been removed from my eyes."

"You should speak with the police," said Holmes. "Inspector Lestrade is your man. He will look out for your interests, as will I."

Bartholomew blew out his candles one by one and then accompanied us down the stairs and to the front door. When we were on the other side of it, he said that he had forgotten something important, and would be right back. Something about the way he had spoken raised an alarm with me. I started to speak, but Bartholomew dashed back into the house and slammed the door shut before I could react. I heard the sound of the bolt being shot.

A thrill of fear went through me.

Holmes, too, was galvanized. He threw himself against the door, but it would not yield.

"Sholto!" he shouted. "Open the door. You do not need to do this!"

"Yes I do," came Sholto's voice through the heavy door. "I do not know where the blackmail material is kept. Thaddeus could get loose again and find it. It is in this house somewhere. Best that it all go to ashes, and I with it. I have known for some time that this day would come, and I have prepared for it. Please, stand away from the house. You cannot get back in. Thank you all, especially Miss Mary Morstan, for bringing about this release."

"What is he going to do?" Miss Morstan wailed. "Help him!"

"There is no time!" Holmes shouted, a look of horror upon his sharp features. "Come away!"

As we dashed down the drive and toward the street, we heard a succession of muffled explosions from inside Pondicherry. When we dared stop to turn and look, we saw the house quiver. And then, suddenly, there was a single, much louder, report and every window in the place, so it seemed, shattered at once. Great gouts of flame burst through, illuminating the grounds like a scene from the *Inferno*. The fire writhed and twisted and climbed up the walls to the roof from all sides. In a very short time, the entire structure was ablaze.

Mary Morstan stood in the street, gazing at the conflagration, seemingly mesmerized. I moved to her side and took her hand in mine. If I expected to find her in anguish, I was mistaken.

"I think it is good," she whispered to me. "There was something awful in that house, something bigger than Thaddeus or Bart, something that had infected the both of them. Bart would never have been happy and

Thaddeus will never be good. Now the whole thing is torn apart and the evil has no home. The House of Sholto is dead, and it will never rise again."

I knew that she referred to more than the blazing structure, and I felt that she was correct. The evil of the old man had passed to both of his sons; one of them harbored it, the other railed hopelessly against it. Major Sholto had failed his twin sons, just as Arthur Morstan had failed his daughter and just as my own father had failed Harry and me. Had we become what we were because of those failures, or was the blame our own?

"The police will be looking for you," said I.

"Then it would be well if they found me as soon as possible. I shall go to them and hand myself in."

"An admirable course. I shall be glad to accompany you, Miss Morstan."

"I would not mind it if you called me Mary," she said.

To my surprise, I found her remark exciting. There was more to this young lady than I had given her credit for when first we met.

"Very well," I agreed. "And, in order to maintain a balance, I suppose you must call me John."

She smiled.

The Fire Brigade arrived, and Lestrade and some of his men soon followed.

"So the one we've got hold of is really Thaddeus," said the inspector, after Holmes had apprised him of the tangled situation.

"Yes," said Holmes. "It seems his poor brother has been covering for him for most of a lifetime. But with Bartholomew gone, Thaddeus will have to face the music by himself.

"I made a grave error. The signs I had noticed, the wall panels that had been removed and replaced, I thought Thaddeus had done it looking for the loot. But it was Bartholomew's work. He had rigged the whole house. Dynamite, no doubt, and a few barrels of kerosene here and there. What an ass I have been!"

"Never mind all that, Holmes," said I. "You are not God and you cannot know everything. You knew enough to bring this thing to the only conclusion that was possible. Now you must let it go, or you will drive yourself as mad as the Sholtos were. Let us just salvage what we can, and to hell with the rest."

The conflagration that had razed Pondicherry House was almost extinguished. I felt a smaller, more personal burning in my heart as I watched a police matron lead Mary Morstan away to whatever she must now face. But I would not let it consume me; that much I resolved.

Lestrade shook hands with Holmes and myself and left us. My friend and I stood there under the cold and silent pre-dawn stars for a time. I had the sense that everything had been resolved but nothing had changed. I shed a few tears, but I was not certain who they were for.

Holmes clapped me on the shoulder. "Good old Watson," said he. "Come along now. It is time to go home."

CHAPTER SEVENTEEN

Aftermath

Some weeks after the climactic events in the case, a group of us gathered together between the familiar walls of 221b Baker Street to perform a relaxed and convivial post-mortem examination. My mood was much improved. I could not help but wonder what sort of a person I was to feel so much better after so brief a time. I was a born survivor, it seemed; for better or for worse.

"So Bartholomew Sholto did indeed die for his brother's sins," said Arthur Conan Doyle.

"Yes, and Thaddeus will live on, though he will never again see the outside of a prison," said Holmes. "As for poor Bartholomew, he is forever freed from his own. It occurs to me that some men become inured to prison. In the case of Bartholomew Sholto, the sentence he served for his brother might have been one of the most pleasant times of his life. Think of it! He worked with the other convicts building Wormwood Scrubs. That may seem a dreary occupation to most, but for him, it was one of the few creative activities in which he was allowed to participate. And he did not have to worry about the machinations of his father and brother. Perhaps that's why he created a prison cell for himself in the upper part of the house. He never recovered from the aftermath of the Hallward gold robbery, an event that set a number of sinister doings into motion.

"The case belonged to Athelney Jones, and he arrested Davies and Sholto. As things turned out, it was hardly a feather in his cap, professionally speaking, but I have no doubt that his banking-account benefited.

As Bartholomew told us, he found himself the recipient of a great deal of largesse from the villainous Sholtos.

"When I first began my practice, and started running up against representatives of Scotland Yard, Lestrade was one of the first to admit, however grudgingly, that I had my uses. I believed that Athelney Jones in particular looked down on my talents, but perhaps it was just the opposite, eh? He did his best to keep me at arm's length or further from the truth in this case. He did not look down on me; he *feared* me."

"And it seems his fears were well-grounded," said Doyle. "Were I a criminal, I would do everything in my power to prevent or curtail your involvement in any investigation of my doings."

"And you would fail miserably."

"I have no doubt of that!"

"I've been keeping an eye on Jones for some time," said Inspector Lestrade, as he stretched his legs and took a sip of whiskey. "I knew he was as dirty as they come, but I could never get any evidence. He knew I knew, and tried to get after me in a hundred different ways, to undermine me with our superiors. Somebody higher up was looking out for him, I was sure. I still don't know who that was, and I might never find out. But with the elimination of Thaddeus Sholto and his blackmail ring, and the exposure of Jones, I suppose it's all academic, as they say."

"Do you mean," said Doyle, "that Sholto had blackmailed Jones' superiors into overlooking his wrongdoing?"

"Wouldn't be the first time such a thing has happened, doctor," said the policeman. "And, sadly, it probably won't be the last. But Lady Justice will hold sway for a week or two, at any rate. Sometimes that's the best one can hope for."

"Thaddeus Sholto had a number of agents working for him," Holmes said. "Quite talented at blackmail, every one of them, and I fear that there is no evidence upon which any of them might be arrested. Lestrade has learned that sad truth in recent days. There's a fellow named Milverton who will bear watching.

"Thaddeus went a bit too far when he attempted to blackmail both me and Mycroft with the same information. I suppose my brother made inquiries about him after the business with the late Grand Duke, and Thaddeus learned of it. Fortunately for the villains, Athelney Jones had already been to Mycroft's private suite courtesy of the Grand Duke's death, and had the lay of the land, so to speak. Mycroft is such a creature of habit that it would be simplicity itself to determine when his suite at the Diogenes Club would be unoccupied. Jones later worked up the fire as a means of getting in to conduct a more thorough search. I suppose both Jones and his master were pleased when they found material that could be used against me as well. It was quite a stroke of luck for them, they must have thought. It would keep me preoccupied.

"All of this is speculation; and so it must remain, since I will never have the truth from my brother. It is quite possible that one of Sholto's victims was persuaded to divulge what he knew about Mycroft's past. It is possible that my brother has friends whom he trusts; a practice he will no doubt abandon after this. I believe he numbers Sir Edmund Henderson among his particular cronies; and from what we know, Sir Edmund is acquainted with both Thaddeus Sholto and Athelney Jones. Whether he participated in any sinister doings with them and, if he did, whether he did so willingly or under duress we shall probably never know.

"When did you first suspect that Thaddeus was at the bottom of it?" Doyle asked.

"Ah," said Holmes, "that is perhaps the most curious aspect of the thing. When I learned of Bartholomew's existence and his past crimes, which, of course, turned out not to be his after all, he seemed to fit the mold that had been taking shape in my mind.

"I did not seriously question this hypothesis until I began to think about the portrait I had begun. Watson pointed out the subtly sinister aspect of the thing, and it set me thinking. As Doctor Doyle pointed out, with regard to seemingly irrelevant impressions, something in my mind was giving me a message. It seems my deductive faculty may operate without my conscious awareness. I do at times arrive at conclusions without being entirely certain how I got there, but this...

"I can only conclude that Thaddeus Sholto conveyed his true nature in ways so subtle, indeed, virtually imperceptible, that they did not register on my conscious mind. But something in that great mass that lies submerged beneath the visible tip of the mental iceberg, as it were, deciphered these signals and communicated them while my mind was engaged in a creative pursuit, rather than a logical one."

Doyle nodded. "A German doctor named Franz Brentano once speculated upon the existence of an 'unconscious mind,' which might behave in just such a manner. I understand that he has recanted to a degree, but some of his pupils have taken up the theory."

"Very interesting," said Oscar Wilde. "More than that, utterly fascinating! The man's true inner nature was revealed by a painting. Mister

Holmes, while I find your style just short of deplorable, it seems that you are truly one of the few painters this country has produced who has displayed true genius. And you didn't even know you were doing it! Would that my own labors could be both so effortless and so fruitful."

"It was an incredibly tangled skein," said Holmes, shaking his head. "And my own involvement seems to have made it worse. I am forced to admit that I acted as much upon instinct as upon logic. This flies in the face of what I have worked for years to build. Perhaps I should give fresh thought to my choice of occupation or at least the methods I employ."

"Do you really think so?" Wilde asked. "Remember what Thaddeus said: 'There is nothing more unaesthetic than a policeman.' My apologies to Inspector Lestrade! Do you want my opinion, Holmes?"

"Have I any choice in the matter, Oscar?"

"None whatever. Just listen. You are an *artiste*. When we first met, I had my doubts about you, but you dispelled them without even trying. Suppose this matter had been left up to the police. Suppose Miss Morstan had not consulted you. Thaddeus would have killed her and what would anyone have done about it?

"But your involvement provoked the villains and others; the course of action you suggested provoked poor Miss Morstan to do the things she did, which further provoked the villains, and so on."

Holmes mulled this over for a moment. "You are suggesting, then," said he, "that I am a consummate, if somewhat unwitting, *agent provocateur*. That I had no more control of the proceedings than did anyone else."

"If you like. That's one way to put it, certainly. But there is more to it than that. It became a bit of a chess game, really, with more than two players. Or perhaps a ballet. You were not merely a disinterested observer, Holmes; you became part of the drama. When you became involved in the matter, the shape of it changed, and it took an entirely new course. You and Doctor Watson are men of action. When you involve yourselves in a matter like this, you cannot remain in the wings. The art of the detective does not begin and end in the armchair. You must take the stage at some point, and then you become an integral part of the production.

"In the end, Holmes, you have to admit that you are the same as the rest of us and we are what we are. We have no choice but to play the roles that we have been given. It may seem like a tale told by an idiot, but all the sound and fury signify *something*. Policemen aside, there is nothing more unaesthetic than chaos.

"My point is that you really have no choice, I'm afraid. You must be what you are. You are trapped. Doomed. As am I. As are Watson and Doyle and Lestrade and... yes, Athelney Jones and Thaddeus Sholto!"

"So I am, after all, a cipher," said Holmes. "An element in an equation that will play out as it will, to a predetermined conclusion."

"Not *predetermined*. I should rather say *inevitable*. They are not the same thing. Everything is part of this hypothetical equation, even the products of our own personalities; what some might call free will."

"I still do not quite follow you."

"Well, let me put it in another way. Consider if you will the snow that has made such a pretty mess of the streets."

"Snow?" Holmes said. "What of it?"

"Well, if it wasn't for the snow, how could we believe in the immortality of the soul?"

"What, exactly, do you mean by that, Oscar?"

"I haven't the slightest idea, Holmes. And that is my point."

My friend was silent for almost half a minute. Then he smiled and said, "I do not understand at all. Which means, if I am reading you correctly, that I understand perfectly."

"I believe you do at that, my dear Holmes. You have a unique turn of mind; as, I flatter myself, do I. And I am what I am; I need not even add 'for good or ill.' It is what it is, and if disaster awaits me, I choose to revel in it. You might as well do the same. You shall never be happy otherwise. You must give *Sherlock Holmes* free rein. But keep in mind that he can never know everything."

I remained silent. Though I was quite fond of Wilde, I still disapproved of the danger into which he had put his family with his activities. I did not doubt that he would continue to do so, under the guise of "being himself."

"Well, Doctor Watson and Doctor Doyle," said Holmes, "it seems that Oscar has cleared away any objections I might have to your chronicling some of my so-called 'adventures.' Perhaps detection is not such an exact science after all."

"Then you give your approval, Holmes?" said I.

"I might as well. If you think there is something in it, and if you can benefit from it, I would be a miserable friend indeed if I stood in your way for the sake of my own vanity.

"One caveat, though, I would not recommend that you use our recent adventure as the subject of your efforts."

"Certainly not," said Doyle. "Though it is a pity."

"That it is," Wilde agreed. "What a fascinating subject it would make! Why, one would hardly know where to begin."

"Not at all, I'm afraid," said Holmes. "Doctors, I would recommend that you expand upon Watson's brief account of the Enoch Drebber murder in his *Reminiscences*. It features elements of scientific deduction, as well as sufficient melodrama to appeal to the average reader."

"It's a bit short," said Doyle. "Perhaps we could append an account of the goings-on in America that led to the tragic events here in London."

"You would have great difficulty obtaining any first-hand accounts of those goings-on, I daresay. The late Jefferson Hope will be of no use."

"Oh, I'm sure I can come up with *something*," Doyle replied confidently.

The first effort by Doyle and myself was accepted by Ward Lock & Co. in November of 1886, but did not see print until late in the following year.

Beeton's Christmas Annual for 1887 carried *A Study in Scarlet*, the name we had decided upon for our account of the Enoch Drebber murder, after considering and discarding *A Tangled Skein*. Doyle proposed the latter title, but then thought better of it.

"The Drebber killing," he observed, "was scarcely tangled at all, compared to the Sholto affair. *That* was a Gordian knot."

Our work met with indifference for the most part, though it was a greater success than my *Reminiscences*—which is of course the very definition of damning with faint praise.

I might have surrendered my ambitions for good at that point, but Doyle believed in the work and its subject, and resolved to try again.

His opportunity to do so came on the 30th of August in 1889. Joseph M. Stoddard, managing editor of *Lippincott's Monthly Magazine*, hosted a small dinner party at the Langham Hotel. Doyle was one of the invited guests, and, at his request, I accompanied him. Upon arriving, I saw another familiar face, that of Oscar Wilde.

It seemed that Stoddart, who hailed from Philadelphia, in America, had the intention of starting up an offshoot of *Lippincott's* in Britain. Both Doyle and Wilde were being considered as potential contributors.

"It is a marvelous idea," said Wilde, after Stoddart had made his pitch. "And seeing you again, doctors, has suggested to me my ideal subject. The

Sholto affair has been percolating in the recesses of my mind these past four years, demanding to be set free in some form or other. I have given it much thought, even when I did not wish to, and I am hard-pressed to continue resisting its entreaties. The offer of money from our host is, I think, the final straw."

"I was thinking along the very same lines," said Doyle, "which is why I invited Doctor Watson to accompany me. Don't tell me, Oscar, that we are to find ourselves at cross-purposes!"

"I think not. Mine will be allegory, while you may present something as close to the truth as you dare."

And that is precisely what occurred. *The Sign of the Four*, by Doyle and myself, a wonderfully distorted version of the truth, appeared in the February, 1890, number of *Lippincott's*; and Wilde's more fanciful and abstract interpretation of the same events, *The Picture of Dorian Gray*, debuted in July of that year.

Oscar Wilde met his own destruction in 1895. Some say he rushed to embrace it. And there was nothing that Holmes, or I, or anyone else could have done to prevent it. It was a busy year for the detective and myself, and we did not become fully aware of Wilde's plight until it was much too late to render any kind of assistance. Not that there was anything we could have done once Wilde initiated his disastrous libel suit against the Marquess of Queensberry. Just as I had feared, his family suffered greatly, and so did he. I could not find it in my heart to condemn him, as did so many others around the world. He may have been foolish, but he was never malicious, and he did not deserve that which befell him.

In the event, Holmes' prediction regarding Thaddeus Sholto's never again seeing the outside of a prison proved an accurate one, though perhaps not in the way that he had envisioned. Six months after his sentencing, Thaddeus Sholto was found in his cell, dead. The official version of the story was that he had hanged himself using strips of fabric torn from his bedding.

Athelney Jones fared no better. While he was locked up awaiting trial, he was killed in his cell by a convicted murderer whom he had arrested three years earlier. Ironically, Jones' doom was a result of one of the few times he had faithfully discharged his duty as a policeman.

As for Mary Morstan...while I had originally regarded her sudden infatuation for me with a certain wariness, I did remain in contact with her. She had stood trial for her part in the crimes of Thaddeus Sholto, receiving a sentence of three years at Her Majesty's Prison Holloway, in North London. She had accepted this without hysteria; in fact, I do not believe she shed a single tear, which endeared her to me all the more. Many letters were exchanged, and there were visits. Well before she was to be released, an informal and largely unspoken understanding had developed between the two of us. Holmes, oddly enough, did not discourage me.

"She is an unusual young lady," he said to me one day. "She has had her share of problems, some of them arguably of her own making, but I would hesitate to judge her harshly. It is plain that she feels drawn to you and you to her. Strange as it may sound, coming from such a 'cold logician' as myself, I would advise you to follow your heart, Watson. It is, perhaps, the only bright spot to emerge from the whole sordid mess."

"Holmes, are you ill?"

He laughed.

"Perhaps I am, in my way. If so, there is little hope for any recovery. But *you*, Watson... I know that you idealize Doyle's home life and that your anger toward Wilde comes from his rather cavalier attitude toward his own. And it is plain that you are drawn to Miss Morstan. I know also that there are problems there, old fellow, but has there ever been a situation that was free of them?"

"She... is not well, Holmes. In fact, she may not have very long to live. I have not spoken to you of this, but... Miss Adler arranged for a specialist to visit Miss Morstan at Holloway. He discovered that she has a brain tumor. How long it has been there, he cannot say, nor can he predict with any confidence what it will do. It is his opinion, however, that Mary, Miss Morstan, should not count on living for another ten years, perhaps no more than five. Further examinations will be made, of course, but modern science knows so little of the brain and the maladies to which it is vulnerable. I fear that the poor woman does not have much longer. She will be released from prison within the year, and I doubt that she will last much beyond that."

"It would be a shame, then, if she were to spend her final years alone. It would also be a shame if you turned your back on her, since you so clearly do not wish to."

It had occurred to me that Holmes was perhaps a bit enamored of her himself. He spoke of her in terms that were respectful, if not reverent. "Her actions," he had remarked to me on one occasion, "were a chaotic blend of madness and brilliance, further complicated by sheer happenstance and still I was able to follow them, to a degree. She was both opponent and ally, and she may well possess the most remarkable mind I have ever encountered." It was the most effusive statement I had ever heard him make about a woman.

"I do have strong feelings for her, Holmes," I admitted. "They came upon me gradually, but they are now undeniable. However, there are complications. The specialist said that she would not suffer any physical incapacitation until shortly before the end. We could have our little bit of happiness, I suppose. But she has, after all, disgraced herself, and..." I let my words trail off, for I knew not how to complete them.

"And *what*?" Holmes pressed. "I know you do not care about that, Watson. And, as you have neither kith nor kin in England, there is no one before whom you need feel shame."

I shook my head. "It's not an easy thing, Holmes. I was brought up in a certain way, after all."

He remained silent for several minutes after that. There was something in his face that I had never seen before. I could not imagine what thoughts he was entertaining. When he spoke again, his voice, too, displayed qualities that were new to me. There was gentleness and pain and...so it seemed to me...deep understanding.

"I know that you are curious about the contents of a certain missive I received during the Sholto business," said he. "I know also that you would never presume to ask about it.

"I am, as you have remarked before, a private man, one who does not wear his emotions upon his sleeve. But that doesn't mean that I don't have them.

"I'd like to tell you a story, Watson. It is a story about a young woman who came from a good family. A young woman who grew up free from want and learned how to behave as a proper lady ought to.

"She made a very rational decision not to follow her heart. She turned down the marriage proposal of a young man whom she loved, and accepted the proposal of one that she did not, because it was, according to her family and her upbringing, the *right* thing to do.

"But she was never happy. Years later, she became involved in an affair with a man who had been hired to tutor her youngest son in mathematics. Her husband learned of this and he murdered her."

He fell silent, his tale told. I thought about it for a while and began to wonder. There was no doubt in my mind about the point my friend wanted to make, but there was something about the story itself... I mustered my courage and put to him a question:

"Holmes, were... *you* the young man she turned down?"

He looked at me as though I had inquired whether he had been born on the planet Mars.

Laughing a little ruefully, he shook his head and said, "No, Watson, I was not. Nor was I the murderous cuckold, before you ask me that. The young lady was my mother. The man who murdered her was my father."

I was too stunned to speak.

"That is the shameful secret of the family Holmes," said my friend. "That is the information Thaddeus Sholto used in his attempt to blackmail me and Mycroft as well, I think.

"Over the years, I have largely ignored it, though I have begun to wonder if it did not perhaps influence my choice of career. I always put it down to my peculiar turn of mind but have I secretly been attempting to atone for the sins of my father?

"Mycroft has worked hard to keep the information suppressed. His position with the government has made it possible for him to expunge all mention of the murder from the official records. But he kept the information near to him, in a place that was not difficult for the miscreants to find.

"On the one hand, it is difficult to imagine him not telling any blackmailer to go to the devil, where matters of state are involved. Perhaps he had faith that I would see the business through to a satisfactory conclusion, just as I must assume that he managed things on his level. I shall never know the truth from him, but I would like to believe that.

"Well, it is a family matter after all, one he has spent many years keeping watch over. He is several years my senior and I do not to this day know what he knew of our mother's... activities. I do know that it hit him harder than it did me, and that his dogged misanthropy seems to date from the incident. Do any of us truly know one another, Watson? Can any of us say

"That is the shameful secret of the family Holmes."

with any certainty what a friend or even a brother will do, given personal circumstances of which we know but little?"

It was unusual to find Holmes in such a philosophical mood, and it was rather infectious.

"Indeed not, Holmes," I said. "In fact, I cannot even say what I myself would do, or *should* do. I seem to be pulled in different directions, but I know I must settle on a single course."

Which, of course, I did. Mary Morstan and I were wed in 1889. It was not what I would call the happiest of unions, but it was gentle and free of recrimination. Her condition gradually worsened, and she passed away late in 1892.

Did I truly love Mary? Yes I did, in my way. But more than that, I felt a sense of obligation, and even a strange sort of kinship. She was alone in the world, as was I. My brother and I had never been close, but his passing had left a void just the same. Poor Mary helped to fill it for a time, though I was doubly empty when she finally slipped away. Or perhaps I should say trebly. Mary's death was my second great loss in as many years, since Holmes had apparently perished in his final confrontation with Professor Moriarty in 1891. For a time, I emulated my brother Henry and took to drink. But the watch served as a reminder of the destination that lay at the end of that road.

After two or three embarrassing incidents, I pulled myself together and, with a bit of help from Arthur Conan Doyle, re-established my medical practice. By the time Holmes "returned from the grave" in 1894, I was a practicing physician, and had begun once again to collaborate with Doyle on a series of short tales for the Strand magazine. The first of these appeared shortly after Holmes' bogus demise. I participated actively in the writing and editing process until Mary passed away. After that, Doyle worked alone, basing his accounts on my extensive notes and his own wonderfully practical and plausible imagination.

Some weeks after the Sholto affair had drawn to a close, I found the courage to broach a subject that had been on my mind.

"I have noticed something, Holmes, and I wonder if it has somehow escaped your vaunted observational powers. I believe Miss Adler has taken an interest in you."

He laughed. "I shouldn't wonder. As Doctor Doyle has pointed out, I am a most fascinating character."

"I'm serious, Holmes. You claim to be immune to feminine charms, but I have my doubts on that score. She is a most interesting woman."

"Now, *there's* a word," said Holmes. "*Interesting.* The Chinese, I think, approach it in the right way. 'May you live in interesting times,' they say when they wish to place a curse upon someone."

"She is a most attractive young lady," I persisted, "and very clever to boot."

"Too clever by half, Watson. I should never be able to get away with anything if I had her for a wife."

"That may be a good argument in her favor."

As I said this, my eyes involuntarily cut over to the corner of the mantelpiece. I saw that Holmes' small morocco case was not there.

He chuckled. "Yes, old fellow, I have put it away. I have learned a valuable lesson from our recent experiences. There is mystery inherent in everything. I need not wait for London's criminals to make a bold move before I can exercise my mental powers. "The proper study of mankind is man,' Watson, and that aphorism holds true for everything else under the sun. There is material enough for me in every waking moment. And if I can find no external mystery to occupy me, there are always the riddles inherent in my own being.

"Drugs are rather cold comfort after all, Watson. I believe I may dispense with them. When London's criminals fail to provide stimulating diversions, for me there still remains…Sherlock Holmes."

THE END

AFTERWORD
by Chuck Miller

In 1970, Trevor H. Hall first advanced the theory that Sherlock Holmes' mother had been murdered by his father. (*Sherlock Holmes: Ten Literary Studies*)

Holmes' offhand remark in the present manuscript that Violet Holmes had been unfaithful with "a man who had been hired to tutor her youngest son in mathematics," is most interesting in light of William S. Baring-Gould's contention, in *Sherlock Holmes of Baker Street: A Life if the World's First Consulting Detective*, that young Sherlock Holmes' mathematics tutor had been none other than Professor James Moriarty.

It seems that Baring-Gould was correct in his surmise that Athelney Jones was a criminal, but he pinned the wrong set of crimes on the "bent copper." As we have seen, Jones would have been in no position to have committed the 1888 Whitechapel murders that have been attributed to the unidentified killer known only as Jack the Ripper. Who the Ripper really was, and whether or not Sherlock Holmes had a hand in the case, are questions for which we may never have definitive answers.

ABOUT OUR CREATORS

AUTHOR –

CHUCK MILLER - was born in Ohio, lived in Alabama for many years, and now resides in Norman, Oklahoma. He is a Libra whose interests include monster movies, comic books, music and writing. He holds a BA in creative writing from the University of South Alabama.

Chuck is the creator/writer of TALES OF THE BLACK CENTIPEDE, THE INCREDIBLE ADVENTURES OF VIONNA VALIS AND MARY JANE KELLY, THE BAY PHANTOM CHRONICLES, and THE MYSTIC FILES OF DOCTOR UNKNOWN JUNIOR. He has also written stories featuring such classic characters as Jill Trent: Science Sleuth, Armless O'Neil, The Griffon, and others.

Miller received the BEST NEW WRITER OF 2011 Award from Pulp Ark. His first novel, the critically acclaimed "Creeping Dawn: The Rise of the Black Centipede" was published in 2011 by Pro Se Press. The second installment in the Black Centipede series, "Blood of the Centipede" was published in 2012. "Black Centipede Confidential" was released in 2013. Also out in 2013 was "Vionna and the Vampires," the first installment of "The Incredible Adventures of Vionna Valis and Mary Jane Kelly."

http://theblackcentipede.blogspot.com/

INTERIOR ILLUSTRATOR

ROB DAVIS - began his professional art career doing illustrations for role-playing games in the late 1980s. Not long after he began lettering and inking, then penciling comics for a number of small black and white comics publishers- most notably for Eternity Comics, which eventually became Malibu Comics in the 1990s, on their book SCIMIDAR with writer R.A. Jones. Branching out to other black and white publishers and eventually working at both DC and Marvel Rob worked on likeness intensive comics like TV adaptations of QUANTUM LEAP and STAR TREK's many incarnations mostly on the DEEP SPACE NINE comics for Malibu. At Marvel he worked on the Saturday morning cartoon adaptation PIRATES OF DARK WATER.

After the comics industry implosion in the late 1990's Rob picked up work on video games, advertising illustration and T-shirt design as well as some small press comics like ROBYN OF SHERWOOD for Caliber. Rob continues to do the occasional self-published comic book as well as publisher and designer for his small-press production REDBUD STUDIO COMICS. Rob is Art Director, Designer and Illustrator for the New Pulp production outfit AIRSHIP 27 partnered with writer/editor Ron Fortier. Rob is the recipient of the PULP FACTORY AWARD for "Best Interior Illustrations" in 2010 and 2015 for his work on SHERLOCK HOLMES: CONSULTING DETECTIVE and has been nominated for the same award every year since the award's inception. He works and lives in central Missouri with his wife and two children.

COVER ARTIST

MAL EARL - is a self taught writer/illustrator based in the scenic Lake District of Northern England. His creator owned, BULLETPROOF NYLON project was the focus for 2015, and a selection of short tales are available online at http://www.bulletproofnylon.com. A series of BPN pulp novels are currently in development, with the first volume set for completion by October, 2015 and a digital comic strip, expanding the saga, began in November, 2015 with Volume 19 of David Lloyds digital comics anthology ACES WEEKLY in November. http://www.malearl.com

www.ingramcontent.com/pod-product-compliance
Lightning Source LLC
Chambersburg PA
CBHW051134260626
47170CB00005B/1806